NO TRESPASSING

KD ROBICHAUX

No Trespassing Production Crew

Editing by Hot Tree Editing
www.hottreeediting.com

Cover Design and
Formatting by Pink Ink Designs
www.pinkinkdesigns.com

Cover Photography by FuriousFotog
www.onefuriousfotog.com

Special Thanks

Cassy Roop of Pink Ink, and Golden Czermak, the Photo Ninja and FuriousFotog himself, y'all are truly a dream team, and I'm so proud to call you my friends. You are both an inspiration to me to stick with something I love doing and to never give up. You two take my breath away with every new cover you create for me, and they just keep getting better and better!

DEDICATION

To Don Wildman, host of the Travel Channel's Off Limits.
May everyone know you are the inspiration for
Dean Savageman, host of the
Adventure Channel's No Trespassing.

ALSO BY KD ROBICHAUX

Now Available:

The Blogger Diaries Trilogy:

Book 1: *Wished For You*
Book 2: *Wish He Was You*
Book 3: *Wish Come True*
The Blogger Diaries Trilogy Boxed Set

Standalones:

No Trespassing

Coming Soon:

The Confession Duet:

Book 1: *Before the Lie*
Book 2: *Truth Revealed*

NO
TRESPASSING

ONE

Emmy

"I HATE HIM!" I HISS, BEFORE tipping back the shot glass of icy Patron, biting into my lime as if I was tearing into the man in question's throat.

"Hate is such a strong word, honey," Erin says, handing me a napkin from beside her, where we're sitting at the bar of our favorite little pub, only a block from the townhouse we share.

And then our usual back and forth begins, as I rant, "That good for nothin'—"

"He's one of the leading historical preservers in the world."

"—selfish—"

"He donates half his millions to charity."

"—asshole! I hate his stupid face!" I finish, ignoring her interruptions, especially what comes out of her mouth next.

"You mean his perfect, drool-inducing, panty-wetting, heart-stopping face?"

All I can do is growl and give her a death stare as I shoot back the next ounce of tequila.

"Come on, Emmy. Even you have to admit how hot he is, whether he is your self-proclaimed mortal enemy or not. I bet 90 percent of the people watching his show are women who only tune in because he's so fucking gorgeous." She takes a sip of her Seven and Seven. "Have you seen his Twitter followers and Facebook friends? Really, like that many hot chicks are watching The Adventure Channel for the history documentaries," she scoffs.

I look at her sideways, feeling my body sway a bit on my stool. "What are you trying to say? Hot chicks can't like history? I like history, you twat. Am I not hot?" I snarl my upper lip at her and cross my eyes, making her laugh. I'll do just about anything to get her off the subject of how good-looking Dean Savageman, host of the popular *No Trespassing* television series, is, because as much as I despise the fucker, I can't deny that man was blessed by God himself in the looks department. The ass.

"Oh, yeah. And you'll be even hotter when your face gets stuck like that." She nudges me with her elbow, causing me to almost fall off my seat.

"Every time, Rin. Every. Damn. Time. I show up at these locations, my hard earned History and Archeology degrees in hand along with my Louisiana driver's license to prove I'm not a terrorist there to do any sort of damage to the place, and no one will let me in. Even name-dropping my freakin' parents won't work. I mean, what good is being the only daughter of pretty well-known archaeologists if it's not going to get me access anywhere?" I huff, only half-joking. "I was conceived against the door of the queen's chamber of the Great Pyramid of Giza, for fuck's sake. Mom and Dad love telling me *that* story." I roll my eyes.

Erin giggles as she sips from her straw. "What did you say the pharaoh's name was again? Coffee something?"

"Ugh, bitch. Khufu." I take the last shot in the row of five shot glasses I'd ordered when we first sat down.

"Yeah, that guy. I bet he rolled over in his pretty coffin thingy," she says, nodding at the bartender for a refill.

"Sarcophagus. You're killing me." I press the ball of my hand to my forehead to relieve some of the pressure I feel building at my best friend's cluelessness when it comes to what I know so much about. But I don't blame her. When she starts rattling on about the newest trends in psychology, I can feel my eyes roll into the back of my head.

"I mean, if I had any desire to go to Egypt and work over there with my parents, I know I'd be set. But growing up surrounded by nothing but images of pyramids, sandy deserts, hieroglyphics, the Sphinx… it's like I'm jaded. That shit doesn't interest me. They submersed me in it too much. I want to see things right here. Right in our country. Shit, right in our state! But no. No one gives a rat's testicle that my mom and dad are the people who drove the crawler robot that discovered that behind the queen's chamber door was yet another door, and that on the other side of that door were hieroglyphs written in red paint. A giant discovery, *huge*, in fact, but apparently meaningless when it comes to getting me access to snap a couple fucking pictures for my blog."

"Tits," she proclaims, and I look at her oddly. "Have you tried showing the security guards your tits? You have great tits, Em."

I start to deny it, but confess, "There was that one time. But it was right here in New Orleans, and I was just trying to get in to watch them add someone to a family tomb in Lafayette Cemetery." I pout.

She looks at me in horror. "There is something so wrong with you. I can't wait until you finally give in and let me shrink you. I'd have a field day."

"No, you don't understand. It's so cool. It's so hot here in NOLA, and the tombs are above ground, like an oven on top of a hole. They put the deceased into the pretty tomb part you see, and then nature does its thing. Then when someone else in that family passes away, they go in there and basically just scrape the remains to the back, where they fall into the hole beneath, and—"

"Stop! That is way too much information. I could've gone my whole life without knowing that," she cuts me off, visibly shuddering.

Even after all these years, growing up with my sweet-natured friend, I always seem to forget she doesn't find morbid things like that fascinating the way I do. I guess it comes from being taught in great detail at a very young age, the process of mummification. I get back to what I was originally talking about so she can quit being grossed out.

"It's just not fair, Rin. I can't count how many times I've been somewhere, practically on my knees begging for just five minutes inside one of these locations, and being rejected, and then in waltzes *Dean*." I say his name like it tastes bad on my tongue. "He walks right in. Doesn't even have to show a fucking visitor's pass. And I swear to God, he smirks at me. He. Fucking. *Smirks*. It's not just in my head." I start to tick off some of the locations on my fingers. "The limestone quarry in Louisville, Kentucky, when that bastard got to go zip-lining underground. *Underground!* The Redmond Salt Mine in Utah. He got to go up on the roof— the fucking *roof*, Erin—of the Cowboys Stadium, before it was opened for its first game, when all I wanted was a quick picture of the new field. And don't even get me started on Alcatraz." I end this by folding my arms on the bar top and dramatically pound them with my forehead, accentuating my whined, "Not. Fucking. Fair!"

"You'll figure something out. But right now, we just need to get you home," Erin tells me, and I don't even have it in me to argue. I want to get home and into my claw-footed bathtub, where I can soak and have my nightly tradition of exchanging goofy-filtered Snapchats with my blog friends Ricky and Calvin. They're the only guys I know who would notice I'm in the tub and not be creepers and ask for naughty pics, seeing how they're married… like, to each other. I met them when I first started my adventure blog. I had Googled how to work my new website, and their comments under the YouTube video I clicked on were absolutely hilarious, since they were as clueless as I was, as they were starting a blog on their life together. So, after commenting with them on there, we became friends on Facebook, and the rest is history. Their friendship is invaluable, and I don't know what I'd do if it weren't for their amazing senses of humor and optimistic outlook on just about everything to brighten my day.

Our little pub has three-dollar You-Call-Its until 11:00 p.m., so I leave a twenty-dollar bill under my five shot glasses and allow Erin to hook her arm through mine and lead me through the door. A five-minute walk down the cracked sidewalk of our narrow French Quarter street carries us past quaint row houses, several with doors propped open, the owners sitting out on the steps enjoying the nightly relief from the humid summer weather. It's still hot outside, but with the sun tucked away for the night, it's our only chance to get a little fresh air without melting. The never-ending sound of jazz music floats on the gentle breeze from the many bars in our area, Bourbon Street being only a few roads over. But also riding along on that draft is the familiar funk of our one-of-a-kind city. It's broken up though by the smell of spicy Cajun food, and occasionally something sweet, maybe beignets, or the delicious scent of coffee.

As we come upon the creole townhouse where we live, I pause in my steps to admire the gorgeous three-story brick building with its wraparound black cast-iron balconies. I always have to stop and appreciate the architecture that seems to make my soul sing with joy. The home has been in my family for generations. With my parents always gone overseas, I stayed with my grandma to finish up school here. And after she passed away at the end of my senior year of high school, when Mom and Dad found out I wanted to stay for college too, they insisted Erin move in with me. Which was fine by me. She'd had hundreds of sleepovers with me since we were kids, so it wasn't any different. Just a little quieter without Granny blasting her QVC and 'stories' 24/7. We'd tried to get her earbuds once, but that didn't go so well after she got up to refill her sweet tea without pulling them out first. Poor old woman nearly had a heart attack as the TV crashed to the floor behind her. After that, we just dealt with the dramatic music of *Young and the Restless* and the constant tune of "Yours for eight *easy payments* of just $19.99!"

"You all right?" Erin asks, bringing me out of the memory.

I look at her and sigh. "Yeah, that's just a loooot of stairs." We both turn our gazes up to the top floor, where our bedrooms glow from lamps in the windows.

With a snort, she pulls on my elbow. "Drinking night ritual before bed. Come on."

We walk up to the front door, the second floor balcony overhead casting a shadow until we get close enough for the motion detector lights to click on. As she closes the door and locks up behind us, I walk down the hall feeling like I'm on a cruise ship as I sway between the narrow walls. Turning into the kitchen, I go straight to the cabinet where we keep the world's supply of Tylenol, as Erin pulls our two giant metal tumblers with straws down from another and proceeds to fill them with water from the fridge door. After a few moments of struggling with the Emmy-proof cap, I finally manage to shake out four of the white tablets before replacing the bottle in its spot.

I hold my hand open to her and she takes two out of my palm after handing me my tumbler. Lifting the pills between us in her fingers as I do the same, she sings, "Here's to you. Here's to me. And here's to the boys who lick us where we pee!"

I throw my head back and laugh. Every time we go out for a drink, this is our tradition. Two Tylenols followed by an entire glass of water after exchanging a hysterical toast, ending the night on a happy note. We've woken up with way fewer hangovers since we started doing it, making it an almost superstitious thing for us. Like when Erin decides to go home with some hottie from the bar, before she actually goes to sleep, the bitch will call me, no matter how late it is, just to toast me and take her dose and water. The one time I slept through her call, she got a massive hangover that lasted three days, and to this day still blames me for that shit. I blamed it on the six hurricanes she drank before we left the bar, but she'll hear none of it.

We both chug our water then move to the fridge for refills to take to bed. We leave the light above the stove on so we can see our way to the stairs, and as we stand before the bottom one, we look aaaaall the way up the twenty steps to where we can see the first landing, knowing we'll have to climb two more sets once we get up there.

"You ever going to install that damn elevator?" she mumbles. I've threatened to many a time, but alas, it's way too expensive. We've done this multiple ways. We've raced, seeing who could go up the fastest, but our out-of-shape asses ended up almost dying from oxygen deprivation by the second flight. We've tried climbing, with our hands down on the steps above us, essentially crawling up the stairs, which seemed like a good idea at the time, until we woke up the next day feeling like we'd done eighteen hundred pushups. I couldn't lift anything for almost a week. But what seems to work the best for us is what we go with tonight. We hook elbows and each take hold of the banister on either side of the staircase, and start lumbering upward, taking a breather at each landing. Sixty steps later, breathing like we just climbed the Eiffel Tower, we hug, tell each other an affectionate, "'Night, bitch," then part ways, going to our bedrooms on opposite sides of the third floor.

TWO

I PULL OFF ITEMS OF CLOTHING and drop them on the floor all the way to my en suite, knowing full well I'll probably trip on them in the morning, but unable to care, hanging on to the bathroom's doorframe to take off my second-skin jeggings. I get them all the way down past my ankles until they won't go any farther as they turn inside out, still attached to my feet. "Motherfuckers," I growl, trying to step on one leg of the denim and yank myself free, but they won't budge. I plop my ass down on the carpet and take hold of the waistband, having to lie back while I pull with all my might until the stretchy jeans finally let go of their death grip with a pop, slingshotting me right in the face. The back of my head lands on the cushiony shag rug next to my bed as I stare up at my popcorn ceiling. "Is this really my life?" I mumble, panting from the effort, after I'd just caught my breath from climbing the stairs.

I huff my way vertical and grab my phone out of my discarded purse before going into the bathroom to start the faucet at the foot of the tub. When it's full enough, I drop in a vanilla-scented bath bomb, which gives off a satisfying sizzle as it fills the room with its comforting fragrance. I throw my long dark hair up into a knot on top of my head then lower myself into the scalding water, letting out a moan while making sure not to get the cell still in my hand wet. After a few minutes of letting heat soothe my aching body, I unlock my screen and touch the yellow app giving me access to my favorite guys. I scroll until I find my favorite filter, letting the skin-smoothing, eye-brightening effects and golden butterflies that flutter around my head do the work that no amount of makeup would be able to do for my exhausted appearance.

I hold down the circular button to take a ten-second video message. "Evening, my fabulous friends. Hope your day was better than mine!" I give the camera a smooch before the time runs out. I choose their names in my contacts list and send it through.

Within seconds, the purple arrow next to each of their names goes hollow, indicating they've watched my message, soon turning into a purple square to notify me they messaged back with their own videos.

I open Calvin's first, and see him sitting next to Ricky on their couch, their dog Miley nestled between them. "Evening, gorgeous. We're just working on the blog. What happened today?"

I open Ricky's, feeling special that he sends me actual videos. His Snapchat stories only consist of pictures with funny captions. In this one, he's using the filter that makes his eyes look extremely large and his mouth nearly nonexistent, making me giggle. "Emmy doll, how did getting into the scary place you told us about go today?"

I message Calvin back, using the same butterfly filter. *Can this thing just follow me around everywhere I go?* "Ugh, long story. Put your phone where your honey can see so I only have to send this once." The red circle timer fills, so I start a new video message after I send it. "I was so close to getting into the catacombs this time. So. Freaking. Close! But just as the guard was about to let me through…" I send, and then start a new one, this time using the filter that makes my eyeballs completely black. "That *asshole* showed up with the guard's boss, flashing a contract and flaunting the fact he has a camera crew, saying he was there to set up marks before they start filming tomorrow." I add a red-faced angry emoji to the top of my message before sending.

When I open Calvin's snap, both of their handsome faces are in the shot. Ricky speaks first, "That dirty, delicious jerk. How does that sexy douchebag keep thwarting your plans for adventure?!" I see Calvin roll his eyes before the video cuts off and then starts again automatically.

"Honey, this is like, what, the sixth time he's done this? We've gotta come up with a plan to get you in," Calvin says, sympathy and determination lacing his voice. His next video comes in, a smiling devil emoji in the bottom left corner of his shot. "You've tried every legal way of getting into one of these places. I say it's time to play dirty."

When my list of contacts comes up, I see Ricky has sent me a snap of his own, his head turned to look beside him. "Ooo, hubby. I love it when you go all naughty boy on me." He faces his camera. "I agree. Time to break out the gloves, sister."

I blow out a long breath, thinking about what they're suggesting. Would I have the balls to do something that could possibly land me in jail if I got caught? I had told them a few weeks prior about the underground catacombs of New Orleans. Not too many people knew about them, because it wasn't a famous tourist location like the ones in Paris. I hadn't believed they even existed at first. I thought it was just part of a ghost story Gran had made up to scare me into keeping curfew. But sure enough, about a month ago, after being paired up with one of the more colorful and eccentric ghost tour guides in New Orleans, when my cousin Jamie came to visit, I managed to confirm they were real after our exploration of St. Louis Cemetery Number 1. The guide, René, an aging man with weathered skin and a shock of white hair under his tall top hat, seemed excited to answer my questions, after I had pulled him aside to ask him if he'd ever heard of the NOLA Catacombs.

"Ah, *chère*," he began in his delightful Cajun accent. Luckily, it was light and easily understandable. "I have, and it's true! Not many people be knowing about it, but I do, and I know where to find it."

My eyes had widened and I looked at him questioningly, and then, he'd taken his hand and pointed downward. I had glanced at the ground and then back up into his smiling face, his eyes twinkling with mirth.

"You're standing over it, *ange*. St. Louis Cemetery 1 be the oldest cemetery in N'rleans, but there was one here before it that just don't exist no more. St. Peter Cemetery. Back in the day, we're talking when the city was still brand new, in the middle of the 1700s, they buried them under the ground, like most normal cemeteries now do, but then the people started thinking it was bad for their health and they built up a big wall." He expressed just how big by spreading his arms wide and flapping them above his head. "Then after a while, when the ground got all filled up with the dead, what everyone *thought* they seen was them covering the ground in lime. Oh sure, sure. They was making a show of building over the top of it, but it was all a distraction of what was going on underneath it all. Have you ever heard about the catacombs in Paris?"

Of course I had. No one in the field of archeology had not learned about the Paris Catacombs. I had done a report on them in one of the earlier classes of my college career. But the stories never got old, so I let him tell his tale. "A little," I prompted.

"Paris is old. Much, much older than anything we have here in the US. So old, it's hard to fathom. And being that old, it's gone through generation after generation of people, all them people fighting wars, fighting plagues, or growing old, and then dying. Millions upon millions of 'em. The graveyards would fill up, over and over again. They had to do something with the bodies. So what they do? After a certain amount of time in the ground, sometimes just enough to let the body break down to bare bones, they'd dig 'em back up again, and they'd move them down into the catacombs to make room for the next."

I knew all this already, but I still listened with bated breath, eager for him to get to the part I was waiting for, when he'd tell me about what was right there, beneath my feet.

He pulled his top hat off his head, ran his fingers through his white hair to scrape it off his humidity-dampened forehead, and then replaced his cover before continuing. "So that brings us back to here, in the late 1700s. They got the bright idea to make catacombs here, trying to plan ahead for overflowing cemeteries. It was before they knew about N'awlins being below sea level, or how they shoulda been burying the people in tombs above ground the whole time. So, while all the people of the early city felt relieved they was getting rid of the burial ground about a block thataway,"—he points in the direction of where St. Peter Cemetery apparently was over two hundred years ago—"they had noooo idea they was getting a burial ground nearly a hundred times the size of it, just about twenty-five feet deeper."

Jamie had yawned beside me, completely uninterested, when I was listening to his every word like it was gospel. I knew she wanted to go home to get ready for a night out on Bourbon Street since she was visiting for her twenty-first birthday, but I asked him the most important of all my questions. "So how do you get down there?"

He pointed to a nondescript two-story building across the street from where we stood. "Have you ever wondered why none of the buildings in this area are taller than that? It's because they didn't know how much weight the ground around here could hold, being hollowed out and all. From what I heard, they was real good about supporting the walls and stuff while they were digging, using some of the lime I told you that they brought in. Anyway, inside that building, there ain't nothing but a desk and a guard. The entrance is in there."

I turned to face the structure in question. I had never noticed it in the twenty-four years I lived here. A simple brick building with a couple of undecorated windows and a front door with a mail slot. There wasn't even a number on it to indicate its address. No hours of business sign, no nothing. When I turned to thank the tour guide for his help, he had disappeared.

A few days later, with copies of my credentials and camera bag in hand, I had gone to the building and knocked on the door. With there not being any type of contact information, not even a business name, that was the only thing I could do. I knew the street number had to be 307 because 305 and 309 sat quaintly on either side of it. One looked to be a sex shop called Pandora's Box, and the other was a New Orleans souvenir store. When I Googled the address, nothing came up, not even any property owner information. Very strange.

At first, there was no response. But with determination and hope running through my system, I stood and continuously knocked on that door until my knuckles went numb, and finally, a giant hulk of a man opened, looking down on me from his well over six foot height. "What do you want?" he grouched.

"Hi there!" I chirped, high-pitched with my excitement

someone actually answered. "My name is Amelia Crain, and I run an archaeology blog called *Unearthed: Emmy Spills the Dirt.*" I held up a printed picture of the blog's homepage to show him. Before he had a chance to close the door on me, I switched documents in my hands and held my degree in front of his face. "I'm an archaeologist and would like information and to book an appointment to enter the NOLA Catacombs to document and photograph for my blog." I decided to go with confidence, as if I did this all the time. Instead of asking with a plea in my voice, maybe requesting with self-assuredness would get me better results. The difference between 'May I?' and 'When can I?'

"I don't know what you're talking about," the ogre growled, and began to shut the door.

"Wait!" I cried, and locked my elbow as I pressed my palm to the wood. He sighed, but reluctantly opened it back up, his eyebrow arched. I felt what little patience he may have running out quickly, so I went with desperation. "Please! I know they exist, and I know the entryway is in there." I stood on my tiptoes to try to see over the massive man's frame, but he blocked all view with his towering bulk. "I swear I won't touch anything. I just want to take a quick look around, snap a few pictures, and then be on my way. That's all! Please." I sighed tiredly before going on. "You don't understand. I've been to so many places all over the states, and the only places I can get in, even after years and years of college, are the same places any Joe Blow can pay for a guided tour or a ticketed entry. I want to document the places that are off limits to most people, report on the things hardly anyone knows about. Please!"

He stared at me with a bored look on his face, but after seeing the growing hopelessness in my eyes, his softened just a fraction. "Look, I'm not allowed to let you down there. Even if I wanted to sneak you in, you reporting on it and posting it all over the internet would get me fired. Nobody gets down there without going through me, so that shit would come straight back to me."

"Please, I..." My words trailed off and I glanced away. I knew begging wouldn't get me anywhere, and I felt my heart breaking at another failed attempt, and realizing my dream would once again be unfounded.

"How about this? We've got some big shot TV show guy and his crew coming in a few weeks," he began, and my hackles rose at the same time my hope did. "When they come and I show them around, I'll take your camera down there with us and snap you some pictures. When you post them on your blog, you can just say one of the crewmembers leaked them to you."

It wasn't the same. I wouldn't be able to truly describe everything from the catacombs, the way it smelled, the feel of the air that deep underground, the chills that would send the little hairs on my arms standing on end from the creep-factor I cherished so much. But if it was all I could get, then I would take it. I didn't know how much information I'd be able to get from a few stolen shots, but maybe if I could sweet talk the big man into giving me some facts to go along with them, I might have enough to create an interesting enough blog post. It's not like this was one of my moneymaking posts; this was more of a self-interest piece. Nearly all my others were solicited from tourist spots wanting advertisement. Apparently, an endorsement from the daughter of world-renowned archaeologists was good enough to bring in lots of adventure-seeking history buffs, but not good enough to allow me into the places I *really* wanted to see.

He told me the date Dean Savageman and his crew would be there to start filming, and we set a time for me to bring him my camera the day before. My camera was like one of my appendages. It was an extension of me, and I never went anywhere without it. Did it make me super uneasy to think about leaving my baby in the hands of a stranger for any length of time, even if it was just for one night? Yes. But if letting my precious have a sleepover with the secretly friendly giant meant I'd get a little bit of a scoop on a secret underground piece of history, then I could deal.

Fast-forward to earlier today, when it was time to meet up for the drop-off. I knocked on the door, not making eye contact with the grinning women coming out of the sex shop a few feet away as I fidgeted on my feet, waiting for the security guard to answer. When he did, much more quickly than the previous time, he opened it wider to let me through.

The place was bare. Nothing on the light grey painted walls, and the simple wooden desk with rolling chair that sat in front of a closed door was empty except for an iPad and a paper cup of coffee. This place gave me the creeps more than any burial ground would have. How could he sit here every day? It felt to me like it would be the same as a padded room in a loony bin, or would drive me into one. The guard closed and locked the door behind us then circled his desk and sat in the chair, rolling himself closer, and I pulled the strap of my crossbody camera bag over my head then placed it carefully in front of him. My hand lingered on the black canvas, as if it had a mind of its own and didn't want to sever the connection.

"So, ummm…" I didn't know where to start. I didn't even know his name. I had asked him for it before, but he told me it was best for me not to know so none of this would come back to him. "Thank you for doing this. Is there anything you could tell me about it, to go into my article?"

He looked at me, seemed to think about my question, and sighed. After a moment, he decided to give in. "Almost the entire city's underground is filled with water. It was just by luck that in the 1700s they found this one area that was solid. They dug in every direction until they hit water again, and there, they sealed it off with limestone. The NOLA Catacombs span roughly four blocks, with three main tunnels coming off the large center chamber. At the end of each tunnel is a smaller chamber, in which two are full of bones. The last one hadn't been started on when the city decided it was much too dangerous to be down there after a hurricane in the mid-1800s, and they started using family tombs above the ground in cemeteries exclusively for a while."

As soon as he started talking, I broke out the notepad app on my phone and typed everything out while he spoke, nodding as my excitement built. I glanced up at him to ask, "Is there any type of record of who is buried down there?"

He swiped his big paw of a hand down his face then leaned back in his chair. "I can't let you see them, because there are some that are well over two centuries old, but yes. Everyone who had originally been buried in the St. Peter Cemetery is in Chamber 1, and—"

He was cut off suddenly by a phone ringing, and he leaned to the left to pull a cell free from his pocket. "Yes?" he answered abruptly. "Scheduled arrival tomorrow at 1700 hours." A pause. The guard looked at his black G-Shock watch and let out a sigh. "That will be fine." And then he tapped the phone to end the call without so much as a goodbye. Seeming to forget I was there, or maybe he didn't care, he grumbled under his breath, "Cocky fucking prick." When he looked back up at me, I lifted an eyebrow in question. "Seems the big TV star needs to come in early to set up marks before they start shooting tomorrow. He'll be here in an hour."

I felt my face heat with anger and, admittedly, a shit load of jealousy. There I was, finally getting more information from one of these off-limit site guards than I'd ever gotten before, and of course, was yet again thwarted by Dean *fucking* Savageman. It was like he had a built-in radar for when I was about to get the scoop before him, and had the money and power to stop me in my tracks. In the last couple years, we'd crossed paths six times, never actually speaking a single word to one another. Why would he, the rock star of history television, waste time on a nobody like me? The only energy he sent my way that I could tell were cocky smirks as he walked through the doors of record-breaking football stadiums and caves that hadn't been entered since Prohibition ended, basically giving me the bird and singing 'Neener, neener' as he walked by. I never actually knew how he could catch up to me and, for all intents and purposes, cut me in line.

I tilted my head back to look up at the ceiling, letting out a cleansing breath to try to calm my growing fury. "That man is the bane of my existence." I blinked back a couple of angry tears that were trying to form, and then faced the big man behind the desk. "He'll be here in an hour. Sir, you would absolutely make my *life* if you'd let me just take one peek down there. You can keep my camera as collateral and still hold onto it to take the pictures later, that way you know I'll just be in and out. I just want to feel for myself what it's like to be somewhere before that…" My throat clogged, cutting off the many colorful things I've called Dean over the years. "Before he does."

He rubbed the back of his neck like he was thinking, battling internally over his decision that could make or break my sanity. He checked his watch then looked up at me, narrowing his eyes, and I fidgeted on my feet. Finally, sighing in defeat, the guard filled me with more joy than I think I'd ever felt in my entire existence, when he said, "Five minutes. Five minutes, and I never want to see your face again after you come pick up your camera. Understood?"

"Yes!" I couldn't help the hop and clap that echoed in the empty room. Without wasting another moment, I stripped off my purse and jacket, leaving them next to his desk as I followed him when he stood up and went to the door. There, he pulled the set of keys attached to his hip toward the knob, unlocking it.

As we entered the pitch-black area, I held my breath until he reached his giant arm in front of my face and flipped on the light switch, disappointment filling me when I saw it was just another empty office. He closed the door behind us, and I followed him to another door, this one containing three deadbolts above the handle.

I held my breath once more as he used a different key for each of the locks, and suddenly my ears started ringing, as my heart began to pound inside my chest so hard, I thought I might pass out from anticipation. He took hold of the handle and finally pushed it open.

It was the smell that hit me first. I loved that scent. It was nearly the same anywhere underground. I had smelled it first when I went to the Natural Bridge Caverns in New Braunfels, Texas, and then many other times when I'd gone to write pieces for places wanting to attract more tourists. It smelled like earth and nothing else, completely absent of the scents of the city it was beneath. I couldn't see anything, so I took a step closer to the entryway, and just as the guard reached to I assume turn on a light...

A buzzer went off in the room, and the man cursed, slamming the door not a foot in front of me closed as he relocked the deadbolts with warp-speed. He grabbed my arm and I swallowed down a squeak, knowing immediately I needed to be quiet, and let him place me bodily next to the door we had come through only a minute before. He looked at me sharply and placed his pointer finger over his full lips, wordlessly telling me to do what I already planned—to stay completely silent. He reached for the knob and pulled it open, effectively hiding me behind it as I heard another man's voice.

"Nox, there you are. Meet Mr. Savageman."

In the crack between the door and the jamb, I saw a hand reach out before it was shaken by the guard's, who I now knew was named Nox. I'd still take his identity to the grave, since he'd been kind enough that he *was* going to let me into the catacombs. My heart beat rapidly, which I think staved off the disappointment of the opportunity being snatched away after getting so close to fulfilling my dream. Right then, the only thing I could concentrate on was staying hidden so Nox wouldn't get into trouble for my being here. I wouldn't be able to live with myself if it was my fault he lost his job.

"Nice to meet you, Nox." That voice. Goddamn that *freaking* voice. I'd recognize it anywhere. It was the voice that narrated my every dream at night, after I'd fall asleep watching reruns of *No Trespassing*. As much as I despised the man himself, I couldn't help but enjoy the show. After all, Dean was living my dream. My TV rarely left The Adventure Channel, and since I always slept with the television on, turned down low as not to disturb Erin down the hall, it was no surprise that my nightly dreams were filled with my exploration fantasies, sullied only by the fact they were reported by the infuriating man standing not a yard away from me.

My heart continued to pound as I watched the sliver I could make out of him. I had never actually been this close to him before. Some strange feeling started in my chest and made its way down to my stomach as I caught a glimpse of his purposely too-long hair, which was shaved on the sides, flop over on one side of his forehead after he ran his fingers through it. The ever-present perfect scruff along his jaw framed his flawless lips, which I knew hid a set of jaw-droppingly straight, white teeth. If I didn't hate him so much, I'd be able to admit his smile made my heart thump every bit as much as the adventures he went on every week.

"You're early, Mr. Savageman," Nox grumbled in his deep bass voice, and I heard Dean's cocky chuckle.

"Well, on time is late in my book, good man, so… Shall we get started?" he prompted, and I made out the sound of the other man moving toward the front door.

"I've given Dean my set of keys, Nox, so after showing him down to the main chamber, you can still head home at your normal time," the man, who I assumed was his boss, said, causing Nox to obviously react doubtfully in a way I didn't see from my position behind the door, because the man added, "No worries, big guy. Dean assures me he'll keep everything locked up after you leave." I could tell Nox didn't like this new development, as his grip suddenly turned white-knuckled on the edge of the door. "Have a good night." And with that, the man I never got a look at went out the front door.

You could almost cut the tension in the room with a knife. Amid the testosterone battle going on between the two men in the doorway, and the predicament Nox and I were in, keeping me hidden from sight, I seriously wanted to just say to hell with it and run screaming from the room, giving Dean a nut-check on the way out. A swiftly delivered *thwap* to his balls might do the trick to bring him down a few pegs from his high horse. Better yet, just as a *fuck you*, I could've run through the doorway leading down to the catacombs just so I could childishly singsong to Dean, 'Ha-ha! I got here first!' But alas, Nox had triple-locked that bitch up tight.

I was startled out of the fantasy putting a devious smirk on my face when that voice filled the air once again. "I'm going to be down there for a few hours. I'll be gone by midnight at the latest. It's really okay just to leave. I won't disturb anything. I just need to scout the best locations to stand while delivering my lines. We got all the information you and Christopher emailed us about the history, and then we also dug up more, no pun intended." I could practically hear the self-satisfaction in his cheesy joke, and I rolled my eyes, even though no one could see it. Nox clearly wasn't amused either, because Dean added, "Just a little archaeology humor. So… I guess just lead the way and I'll be out of your hair."

I could feel a cold sweat break out on my forehead. What the hell were we going to do? But Nox was on top of it. The towering wall of his back became visible as he opened the door wider and gestured for Dean to enter the room. With my eyes fully alert on his every move, I caught it when the hand holding the door open sent me a signal, his pointer finger silently tapping in the direction of the opening, and just as Dean passed into the room, I slipped under Nox's massive arm, between his hulking body and the door, behind Dean's back.

As the door was closing behind me, I turned back to take one last look at the one I nearly made it through not five minutes before. The one that separated me from a piece of forgotten history I had been so close to rediscovering. But instead, my eyes made contact with the obscenely beautiful blue ones filled with confusion and laughter, which belonged to a man I wanted to throttle, just as the door closed.

I grabbed my purse and jacket from the side of the desk, surprised Nox's boss hadn't asked who they belonged to, chalking it up to him practically fangirling over the TV star who was currently wandering the depths of *my* catacombs, and stormed out of the building, not stopping until I made it to the pub. I had called Erin as I took my first shot of tequila, and she'd shown up only a few minutes later.

It isn't until I suddenly shiver that I snap out of my fuming and realize I'm in a tub full of now-cold water. Toeing the faucet, I put scalding water in to reheat my bath, nudging it off when it's warmed back up.

How had he pulled it off? How did he manage to show up at the exact moment I was about to step through that doorway? I had gotten a single whiff of that sweetly earthy scent wafting up what had to be stairs leading down into the depths of the catacombs. But now I'd never know for myself what lay beyond that wall of darkness, not until I got my camera back from Nox, and then furthermore when Dean's episode of *No Trespassing* aired.

I wonder what he'd do if someone did that to him, dangled something he wanted more than anything right in his face and then snatched it away. But no—no one would dare step on the toes of the rock star of history docs. He wouldn't allow them to.

So what would Dean do? He wouldn't give a rat's ass if it were illegal. He wouldn't be afraid of getting caught. He'd do what he needed to do to make the discovery, to explore whatever site he felt the need to uncover. He wouldn't let anyone or anything get in his way.

What would Dean do?

He'd sneak in fearlessly and brave those depths without anyone's permission or say so.

I sit up with a slosh, and before I have the chance to talk myself out of it, I'm up and out of the tub, drying off and throwing my clothes back on. Even though it's hotter than Hades outside, I wrap my jacket back around my purse strap, a habit from growing up in the south, where they blast the air conditioning, even when you dress for the smoldering heat. I grab a pair of socks out of my dresser drawer and stumble around as I pull them on, having the mind to actually sit on the edge of my bed while I tug on my Converse. With remnants of the tequila fueling my courage, I grab my sequined Pink brand backpack and my tumbler full of water and try to make my way quietly down the stairs.

Moving into the kitchen, I rummage quickly through the cabinets, grabbing handfuls of snacks. I know any minute the drunk munchies are going to start, and I don't want anything distracting me from my adventure. With my backpack stuffed with the world's supply of chips and Little Debbies, I reach into the fridge to grab two white Gatorades and slide them into the side pockets. I am bound and determined to sober up so I can truly take in and remember my first breaking and entering.

I look at the time on the microwave, 11:47 p.m., and head out the door. Dean said he'd be out of there no later than midnight. By the time I get there, he'll definitely be gone, and then I can find a way to get in. I mean, how hard could it be? They make it look so easy in the movies. A little wiggle of one of my bobby pins and I'll be set! But as I walk, my steps hurried in my adrenaline-fueled scramble to get there, my brain starts to see through the tequila, and I wonder if I really will be able to get in.

Maybe this is all for nothing. Say I am able to open the door. Am I really going to break into a secure building, find a way to get past that other door Nox had sealed up like Ft. Knox—I tipsily giggle to myself at that thought—and then sneak around the underground tomb by myself? Will my conscience even let me? My heart gives a thump. At least I know one thing: if I really do get down there, I will be fearless. Unaccompanied in these locations is my happy place. I don't feel alone; I don't feel scared or freaked out like I imagine a lot of people would. I feel free. Free to do my life's work, to soak in every morsel of history left on the walls and in the air, to explore and be uninhibited, to learn the real story of the place then daydream about what could've happened there behind the written retelling.

Before I realize it, lost in my thoughts, I'm suddenly in front of Pandora's Box, the hot pink door bringing awareness of where I am. I glance around, seeing the street is abandoned this late at night. A few streets over, the never-ending party that is Bourbon Street still blares with its jazz music, breaking glass bottles, and people singing and shouting drunkenly. I take out my phone and glance at the time, seeing it's now 12:05 a.m. Perfect. Dean will have already left by now, and with a new rush of adrenaline, I plaster myself to the front of the building, and scoot toward the unmarked door I'd exited several hours ago.

THREE

DEAN

Thirty minutes earlier…

I GLANCE DOWN AT MY GIANT black wristwatch, seeing the glow-in-the-dark hands read 11:35 p.m. I need more time. The catacombs are much larger than expected. So many nooks and crannies to discover. With so little written history on the underground tomb, it's no surprise the ancient hand-drawn map I was emailed is off. But this happens pretty frequently with the forgotten places I choose to take my show. I just need more time than what I had allotted myself with the glaring behemoth who didn't leave me be for another hour after he was *supposed* to leave.

I can't concentrate and let the sites speak to me when someone is watching. That's why I always come a day or two earlier than when we're scheduled to shoot. It sounds corny as fuck, but I wander… *wander* and let the walls talk. I read the facts given to me, and then I walk through the abandoned location, letting it tell me its side of the story.

In a weird way, I feel like they know I'm just like them. Abandoned, forgotten, left to try and survive on their own with no one to take care of them. So they feel like they can open up to me, because we share that same history.

I lie back on the hard-packed dirt floor, link my hands together behind my head as a makeshift pillow, knees and eyes to the craggy ceiling. I guess I really shouldn't complain. Here I am, doing what I love and making money at it. My bit of fame an added bonus. If I hadn't been left at the orphanage within running-away distance of the abandoned coal mines I used to escape to, then who knows how my life would've turned out. I've heard so many horror stories of older kids being taken into the system, so I know I should count my lucky stars there too.

The first and only time I ran away, I spent several hours in that mine, drifting through the tunnels and feeling at home for the first time since my mom dropped me off and hightailed it away in her beater car. It was one of the groundskeepers of the orphanage who finally found me, deep in the dark with only the little keychain flashlight I'd stolen that I found in a toy box, thinking I was gonna run away for good. I had found an opening in the ceiling of the mine, a small metal pipe allowing a pinpoint of sunlight to beam down into the cavern, and I'd laid next to it, fascinated at the tiny dust particles dancing in and out of the ray.

Mr. Watson could've been a complete jerk. Here was this little brat who ran away, and he was sent to find me, keeping him from all the jobs he already had to do around the orphanage. He could've yanked me out of there and dragged me back, kicking and screaming. But no. He didn't say a word. He came and sat down on the ground next to me then mimicked my position, the same pose I lie in right now, and we lay there silently, staring up at the ceiling of the mine, through that little pipe, for I don't even know how long. When it grew dark outside, he pulled a lighter out of his pocket and lit the lantern he'd brought with him, and turned off the Maglite flashlight he'd found me with. I hadn't bothered running. Why waste the energy scampering through mines I knew nothing about, when I knew he'd just catch me eventually?

Finally, he'd spoken. He hadn't scolded me for escaping. He hadn't tried to talk me into going back with him. No, nothing like that. He started telling me the history of this abandoned coal mine, in great detail, from it's discovery, right up until the day it closed, when he'd had to say goodbye to the job he loved, but luckily and happily found another not too far away, taking care of the massive mansion that had been turned into the boys' home. I hung on his every word, listening to the tales he spun, the pranks he and his coworkers had pulled on each other while mining, so easy to picture as we lay there in the setting itself.

No great tragedy had struck. Nothing newsworthy, except for the fact the mine had finally run empty and a hundred miners had lost their jobs, forcing them to move on to the next. And so the mine had been deserted… just like me. And for the first time in the four months I had been there, I cried. The man, probably around fifty years old or so, wrapped his strong arm around my eleven-year-old shoulders, lending me his infallible strength as I cried myself weak. When I ran out of tears, he stood and held out a work-roughened hand, waiting to see if I'd willingly go with him. What he said next changed my life, putting me on a course that would lead me to an unexpected but dream-discovering journey into adulthood.

"Son, come on now. No more running away. This here wasn't the first mine I ever worked. It ain't the only place with history I been, neither. If ya come with me now, I got all sorts of stories I can tell ya."

I had looked from his calloused hand up into his kind and honest eyes, and then after wiping my face full of tears off with my T-shirt, I sniffed one last time before placing my much smaller hand in his. He'd pulled me to my feet effortlessly, slung his pack onto his back, then threw his bulky arm around my shoulders as we made our way out into the night. On our trek through the woods back to the orphanage, at my request, he told me more of the pranks he'd pulled on the other miners, and I laughed for the first time in what seemed like forever.

That was nearly twenty years ago now, and I still remember verbatim the stories Mr. Watson told me throughout the years I spent at the boys' home, until I turned eighteen, used the scholarship I earned to go to UPenn and get my degrees in history and archaeology, all while earning money on the side as a tour guide at their archaeology museum. It was in my last year there that I unknowingly gave a guided tour to a TV producer, who ended up offering me a job to host a documentary on the Ivy League College for The Adventure Channel. The rest, as they say, is history.

I lie here for a few more minutes, taking in the ceiling, how in places it's smooth and nearly perfect, but then textured and almost potholed in others. I let my mind wonder how it was shaped and molded, imagining the first men down here working, digging, if not slaving, given the century it was built and the state we're in. Finally, I check my watch once again and see it's five minutes 'til midnight.

I heave myself off the floor and decide to go above ground to get some phone reception to call Mr. Hosea. I'll let him know I'm staying in the catacombs for a while longer, so not to freak out if he sees the security system hasn't been activated yet. He told me he'd check at midnight from his phone app to make sure I did it right.

I climb the stone spiral staircase twenty-five feet, until I reach the long, more modern cinderblock hallway, and then exit through the triple-locked door Nox allowed me through several hours ago. Through the empty room, then through the entry room with its lone desk… and it reminds me.

Had I not seen her bag sitting behind the desk, the bag she'd carried every time I ran into her, the big bright red one that looks like a typewriter, I would've questioned if I really caught that split-second glimpse of her earlier, as the door shut on her startling green eyes. For a while, I thought she was a figment of my imagination, always showing up at nearly every obscure site I went to. Was she an apparition, a ghost I'd picked up along the way, who followed me everywhere I went? But no. It wasn't until the show took me to Cowboys Stadium, when I got close enough to her that time to hear her grumbled, "Site-stealing dickhead," as I made my way into the brand new football arena to shoot. I nearly stumbled, and turned back to speak to her, but she was being escorted off the premises, her long, dark ponytail swishing behind her, above her perfect, also swishing ass.

Being on a tight production schedule, and now knowing the other times I'd seen her weren't visions of an ethereal beauty, I didn't go after her, figuring I'd see her again. At which point, I planned to ask her who the hell she was, and why she was following me. If it weren't for the colorful name she'd called me the last time I saw her, I would've been worried she was one of the crazy fangirls on my social media accounts. One wouldn't believe what women send me in my private messages. Maybe a vag-pic did it for some men, but not me. And did they really expect me to send them a dick-pic in return as requested?

Which made my beautiful apparition even more intriguing. I'd never experienced a woman not practically drooling at my feet at my every appearance. And not only did she not offer herself up to me on a silver platter or even try to play it cool… oh no, she'd been moderately hostile. Her unreceptiveness made my dick twitch. Then, the half a glimpse I got of her today, the near-hatred in her eyes immediately filled my cock painfully behind the zipper of my jeans. There was no faking that emotion. She wasn't playing hard to get; she genuinely seemed to want to kick my teeth in.

I shake myself, not wanting to think about the psychology behind me getting a raging hard-on from a girl hating me, and hurry out the front door. I pull my cell out of my jeans pocket, and unlock the screen, watching for it to switch from saying *No Service* in the upper left corner. It always takes it a while to sync back up after coming out from underground. I stroll along the sidewalk, listening to the distant sound of jazz music, glancing up when a street-washing truck drives by, filling the street with sudsy water that immediately runs to the sides of the concrete, then flows into the nearest storm drain. Keeps the roads clean, but does nothing for the smell that is New Orleans.

Finally, as I turn the corner, finding the twenty-four-hour coffee shop I was unconsciously searching for, three of the five reception bars light up, letting me know I can text Mr. Hosea.

> *Mr. Hosea, this is Dean. Letting you know I'll be staying a couple hours longer. More to the tunnels than what the maps showed. No reception down there, so I won't be able to respond after this message. Have a good night, and I'll see you in the morning.*

I reread the message, making sure there are no typos—a habit of mine I've had since college—then press send. I figure it'd be better to ask for forgiveness later than to ask for permission, in case he were to actually try to tell me no. Best to avoid that conversation completely.

"What can I get start—" The barista's words cut off abruptly when she turns around and looks up at me. The familiar star-struck look overtakes the young woman's face as she pushes her thick glasses up higher on her nose, probably trying to make sure her vision is perfectly clear. It is this face that always lets me know whether a person watches my show or not. It is the same face on both men and women, but from men, it's because they are passionate about history, not my looks. Well... most of the time anyways. Not that women don't like history or anything, but in my experience, my female viewers seem to enjoy watching *me* rather than learning about the places where I film.

I smile at her like I don't see she's completely in shock at my presence at her counter. "Yes, could I get a large bold coffee to go please?"

"Room for cream and sugar?" she squeaks, almost like she's on autopilot. She hasn't even blinked as she continues to stare at me wide-eyed behind her black-framed glasses.

"Just a little room for sugar please." I watch as she grabs a cup, places it under the large urn marked *Bold*, and then begins to fill it, making me nervous since she's done all this without taking her eyes off of me. I'd feel horrible if she got burned. "Um, sweetie..." I nod toward her hands when the dark liquid reaches the halfway mark.

"Huh?" she says dreamily, then finally breaks eye contact and looks down at the cup, jumping a little when she sees it's almost full. Luckily, it doesn't slosh, and she turns off the flow before it runs over onto her fingers.

She covers it with a lid before handing it to me, and I hand her a twenty dollar bill. When she tries to give me my change, I point to her tip jar and turn toward the counter holding all the coffee fixings, stopping when she whimpers a quiet, "Would you..."

Seeing her phone in her hand, and considering she apparently can't form words, I put her out of her misery. "Sure, babe." And just like I knew she would, she turns and holds her front-facing camera up, life coming back into her features when she grins ear to ear and snaps a selfie with me toasting the picture with my coffee, giving my practiced-to-perfection smile I'm known for.

"Thank you so much, Mr. Savageman! I'm a huge fan! I've never missed an episode! I can't believe you're in N'awlins, in my coffee shop. I can't wait to see what this show will be about. There's so much for you to document here." This all came out in a rush, which is what normally happens after the initial shock fans have when I just show up somewhere wears off. I can't help but smile to myself, thinking what a surprise she's going to have when she realizes that all this time, she's been working above one of the best-kept secrets in US history.

"Make sure to tag me in your picture, okay?" I always ask fans this, enjoying the light that comes on behind their eyes. It makes them feel special. I may come across as a cocky asshole, but I do have a heart… somewhere in there. I know this, because it makes me feel good when I can make my followers grin like I just made their life.

"Oh, I will! Have a good night, Mr. Savageman," she calls excitedly, as I finish pouring sugar into my black coffee, replace the lid, and head out the door.

My phone buzzes before a deep voice growls, "Mail, motherfucker!" letting me know I received a text and making me chuckle. My ringtone never gets old, *Eurotrip* being one of my favorite movies. I pull it out of my pocket and glance at the screen, not bothering to unlock it as Mr. Hosea's message scrolls across my screen.

Anything you need, Dean. Have a good night.

Good man. I'm glad I had him to deal with, rather than the ogre who guarded the door to the catacombs like it held the Fountain of Youth in its depths. I shove my phone back in my pocket right as I reach the door to the unmarked building, pulling it open then locking it behind me, ready to explore the unmapped parts of the cavern two and half stories below.

FOUR

Emmy
5 minutes earlier…

UNLOCKED.

How in the holy hell was this fortress, normally buckled up within an inch of its life behind three doors with multiple locks, left completely open?

Am I that drunk? Am I dreaming? I think to myself, as I slowly, quiet as a mouse, make my way down the long hallway that came after the door I never made it through this afternoon. I keep glancing behind me, thinking this might be a trick. Is someone going to jump out with a camera and yell, "Psych"? Or worse, is there a cop waiting for me at the end of the hall, who as soon as I turn the corner will cuff me and drag me to jail for trespassing on private property in the middle of the damn night? I mean, because technically, it wouldn't be breaking and entering. The front door was unlocked! Of course, I didn't discover this until I tried using my bobby pin to turn the deadbolt like they do in movies, after nearly breaking my credit card in half in the crack by the knob, before becoming frustrated and just jerking on the handle. I nearly busted my ass in the middle of the sidewalk when the door came flying open. But no one has to know that.

My heart thuds in my chest as I tiptoe the last few feet of the hallway, and with my back against the wall, I slowly peek around the corner. I breathe out a sigh of relief when I see no one is waiting there to jump out at me, but then immediately gasp, discovering the spiral staircase leading downward. I feel almost entranced as I walk forward and look down. My first step is hesitant, but as the air becomes thicker and that glorious smell becomes stronger, I end up galloping down the stairs, my hand keeping me steady as it runs along the stone wall, which has a string of lights running all the way down. When I reach the last step, my mouth falls open, and I plop down on my ass.

Tear spring to my eyes; it's so freaking beautiful. The giant gaping cavern is lit by a nearly invisible lighting system, which continues in the distance down three tunnels. It looks much more modern than the strung lights lining the stairs, as if it were put in recently. It would make sense, since they'll need it for the documentary they're about to film.

I sit there for a while, just taking it all in. There's not a single inch of the main room that my eyes don't land on. I wish I had my camera at this moment, but at the same time, it's kind of nice seeing everything just as it is, not through a lens. I'm able to get past not being able to capture everything on film, knowing Nox will be taking some pictures for me later. So for now, I just enjoy the glory of being here.

I've finally done it. I'm actually here, inside a location hardly anyone on the planet knows exists. I'm seeing things that just a handful of people have seen in centuries. The excitement fills me up, boiling over as I jump up from the step, swing off my backpack, sweater, and purse, and start dancing around, pumping my fists in the air and shaking my ass, squawking, "Oh yeah! Oh yeah! I did it! I did it! I did it, did it, did it! Boo-yah!"

I continue my victory dance around the perimeter of the cavern, doing the running man across the radius and back again, all while singing my "Whoop whoop!" and "Can't touch this!" until I'm completely out of breath, and bend forward in the direct center of the room, bracing my hands on my knees as I pant, the grin never leaving my face.

"Well, that was interesting," that *voice* suddenly says behind me, and I let out a scream and fall forward, twisting just in time to land on my side rather than my face, knocking what little air I had out of me. "Oh, my God. Are you okay?" Dean rushes forward, sitting a large paper coffee cup on the ground before coming to bend over me. His hand touches my arm and I jolt. A feeling of static electricity shoots up to my shoulder then down into my chest, setting off what feels like the grand finale of a Fourth of July fireworks show.

What… the fuck? I think, but all that comes out of my mouth is, "Ow."

Before I know what he's doing, Dean scoops his arms beneath me, one behind my back and one under my knees, as he lifts me effortlessly off the ground. I gape like an idiot, seeing the face that begrudgingly haunts my dreams every night, so close to mine.

God, his eyes are even more gorgeous in person. I can see specks of gold throughout his blue irises, reminding me of a cave that hasn't been mined. His nose captures my attention next, making me want to trace down the bridge, where it looks like it might've been broken years ago. The tiny flaw seems to make him even more attractive, seeing he's not as perfect as he looks on TV. My eyes travel downward, landing on his lips. So many days I've woken up, pissed that I'd subconsciously fantasized about that beautiful mouth of his, the bottom lip much fuller than the top, making me dream of nibbling it between my teeth.

The thought pulls me out of my trance, reminding me the man holding me is my sworn enemy, the bane of my existence, the bringer of all my life's frustrations, and I start to wiggle in his grip.

"Whoa, calm down. You're gonna hurt yourself again," Dean says, and it adds fuel to the budding flame that is my temper.

"One, do not *ever* tell a woman to calm down. No one in the history of ever has *ever* calmed down by being told to freakin' calm down. And two—what are you doing down here?" I ask, sounding almost like I have the authority to be throwing out the question. I feel awkward standing there in front of him, having that restless feeling of not knowing what to do with my hands, so I begin brushing myself off, trying my best to ignore those beautiful eyes staring at me as I knock the dust off the hip I'd landed on.

One side of his mouth lifts, along with an eyebrow, as he repeats, "What am *I* doing down here? I think that's a question better aimed at you, love."

"Don't call me that. I meant I thought…" I cut my words off, not wanting to out myself.

His eyes light up with understanding, making me cringe. "Oh, you meant you thought I was supposed to be out by midnight." At my guilty look, he adds, "Yeah, love, I saw you today. You were listening in on our conversation, huh?" When I don't answer, he smirks. "Did we interrupt a little something-something going on between you and the big guy?"

I gasp as my eyes widen. "What? No! I was…" I stop myself again, but I realize it doesn't matter when he starts to chuckle.

"I'm just kidding. I've seen you at enough sites now to know you've been trying to get into one. So tell me, did you make it this time?" he inquires, and I glance away.

Right now, I could totally lie and say I beat him down here, that I'd gotten to see it all first before he showed up, stealing back the glory that was so close to being mine. But the thought of being dishonest about the discovery made my stomach turn. And the idea of lying to Dean himself didn't feel right either, which confused the hell out of me. Who would feel bad about lying to the bad guy in their epic adventure tale?

So instead, I popped my hip, placing my hand on it, as I said as haughtily as I could muster, "Obviously not. You just caught me in the middle of my happy dance, remember? Or are you so used to girls falling at your feet that you already forgot about scaring the ever-loving shit out of me?"

He rubs the back of his neck, looking somewhat guilty, which surprises me, seeing how I always imagine him as being a heartless, cutthroat douche-canoe. "Yeah, sorry about that, love." He clears his throat and a mask seems to pull over his face, and I see the Dean I'm used to viewing on my television screen. Cocky, sarcasm heavy in his voice, he adds, "I was just so enthralled by your amazing dancing ability that I didn't consider you thought you were down here having a solo party in my catacombs."

"*Your* catacombs?" I squawk. "You… I…" I can't even form a sentence I'm so pissed. How dare he call them *his* catacombs? I was here first! I might not have actually been down in them first, but I had been told stories about this place since I was little. I was the first one who showed up at their front door. I was the first one to smell their dense air wafting through that last locked door as it was opened before me. They were not *his* fucking catacombs!

When I finally got the words unscrambled in my head, they came out in a bellow. "You site-stealing, dream-crushing, arrogant bag of dick tips!" I ignored his sharp, quick cough of laughter. "These were *mine*! Everywhere else you got in that I didn't, okay,

I was shit out of luck. I got there first, but you had the power to get in when I didn't. Sucks for me. But this? This is personal, you jerkoff. My Gran told me stories of this place since before I can even remember, and you *stole* them from me! You weren't even supposed to be here yet!"

Absently, I hear a light rumble. They must be scrubbing the road above. It's the right time of night for the trucks to make their passes up and down the one-way streets. My heart pounds in my ears as I try to control my growing anger. Any alcohol left in my system has dissipated by now, my fury burning it off like kerosene. I feel like I could rip Dean's pretty eyeballs right out of their sockets for getting to see my dream site before me.

DEAN

I HAVE YET TO LEARN the name of the beauty before me, but she is absolutely stunning in her fury. She's like an exquisite, ferocious feline, with her snapping green eyes and pearly white bared teeth. As she hisses and spits her angry words at me, I have to reach down to adjust myself before I tent my pants, and her eyes follow the movement, taking her vehemence to a whole new level.

"You did *not* just do that! Are you seriously getting a boner right now?" she yelled, and the small tremor I'd heard previously sounded again.

"Look, you need to calm—"

She cuts me off with a screech. "Ugh! Did I not just tell you never to tell a woman to calm down? How about you un-swell your head enough to where you can actually listen!"

The rumble grows louder, vibrating the ground, and my heart

starts to pound. "Listen to me. Stop yelling. Do you not feel that?" I raise my arms a little, palms facing the ground, trying to center myself and get a feel for the cavern around us.

"It's just the street sweepers. Stop trying to change the subject and answer me! What gives you the right to come down here, calling these *your* catacombs? How do you keep showing up before you're supposed to, thwarting every chance I get to actually make it into a site? *And why the hell are you getting a hard-on, when I so clearly hate your guts?*" she yells the last question, and this time, the ground begins to shake beneath us.

Dirt starts raining down on us lightly, before a rock is shaken loose, causing a downpour of clay and dust. Without even thinking, I scoop up her bags, throw them over my shoulder, and practically tackle her as I pick her up in my arms, sprinting as fast as I can into the closest tunnel. We barely make it through its entry before the cavern starts to collapse behind us.

I keep running, the lighting system flickering in the ceiling. I hadn't had the chance to explore this tunnel, so I pray it leads deeper than the other one I'd wandered just hours ago. The dust cloud that will soon head our way will be a force to be reckoned with if we don't get far enough away from it, and that is not something we want to have to deal with on top of being trapped down here like I know we probably are.

FIVE

DEAN

"I DID THIS. I'M THE MOST wretched human being on the face of the planet," the girl says, repeating what she's been chanting for the last twenty minutes as she sits next to the ceiling-high pile of boulders and dirt blocking the tunnel we ran through. Her cheek rests on one of the rocks as she strokes it apologetically, tears streaming down her now-muddy face.

I don't even have the heart to scold or share in her self-accusations. She's doing enough of that on her own. She looks pitiful right now, completely brokenhearted, and I find myself wanting to comfort her, rather than make her feel worse about what's happened. But I don't dare try to make her feel better. The girl made it perfectly clear what she thinks of me, her disdain literally coming down on top of my head.

So I just sit and watch her pet the boulders, listening to her cry about being the most epic failure in the history of archaeology, praying she doesn't jostle anything loose that could fall down and hurt her. Thankfully, Mr. Hosea had listened to me a couple weeks ago, when I'd told him about the lighting system that needed to be installed for the show. Each fixture is independent, with it's own power source, so we still have light since the whole system didn't get knocked out.

Which means I have the perfect view of her killer figure. The way she sits, pressed up close to the wall of what used to be the cavern's ceiling, I can't help but admire the curve of her ass covered by skintight jeans that encase her thin but shapely legs all the way down to her ankles, stopping at a pair of light pink Converse. The choice in shoe color surprises me. Her feistiness doesn't make her seem like a pink-wearing kind of girl. She comes across more like the blood red of her purse she's got cuddled to her generous breasts.

When I'd finally stopped running farther into the tunnel, after hearing the last of the rumbling die down, I set her on her feet and held her steady by the shoulders while she shook with shock. I knew it was shock, because the first thing out of her mouth when she spoke was, "You saved my Kate Spade," pulling her typewriter-print bag off my shoulder and hugging it to her chest. I mean, I didn't know if it was normal for a woman to name her purse the way a man names his car, but in either case, she had to be in shock if the first thing she worried about in the disaster was her bag.

Moments later, she slowly made her way back in the direction we'd come from, finding the wall of debris, then fell to her knees before it. I would've laughed at her dramatics if she hadn't immediately curled in on herself and started crying her little heart out, and suddenly, surprising the shit out of myself, I felt my own heart breaking for her. My initial response was to run up and put my arms around her, but I thought better of it. It was her hatred toward me that caused all this in the first place. And after the things she yelled at me, I finally understood where the hostility came from for the past couple years.

I'm not too worried, seeing how people know I am down here, and it would only be hours before they discover I'm trapped. As long as nothing else collapses, we can easily survive until they find a way to get us out. But like the girl, I do feel bad about the piece of history being destroyed. Yet, there is nothing we can do about that now, so finally, after hearing her weeping die down a bit, I decide it's time to grow a pair and approach her.

I try to make noise, shuffling my feet and kicking around pebbles as I go, so she can hear me coming instead of surprising her again, and then I squat down next to her. Throwing caution to the wind, I reach out and tuck a strand of the dark hair that had fallen in her face behind her ear, revealing a dirty and tear-stained yet still beautiful face. She glances up at me with her red-rimmed eyes, sniffling as her bottom lip trembles.

Our gazes lock for a moment, making my heart race behind my dark gray zipper hoodie, and I have to fight the urge to kiss her, to distract her from what has clearly hurt part of her soul, knowing she'd caused this misadventure. Then it dawns on me, I still have no idea who she is. So to keep myself from pulling her into my arms and kissing away her broken heart, I speak for the first time since the rubble settled.

"What's your name, love?"

Her watery eyes dart back and forth between mine, seeming hypnotized, as she breathes, "Emmy, short for Amelia. Named after Amelia Earhart, the first female to fly solo across the Atlantic Ocean." It comes out monotone, like she'd told the explanation countless times during her lifetime. "My mom was obsessed with Amelia's disappearance during her 1937 world flight, and said if she ever had a little girl, she'd name her after her hero," she added, blinking up at me then wiping her nose with the back of her hand before looking down into her lap. "Sorry, I ramble when I'm upset."

"No need to apologize, Emmy." I try to put her at ease, which is so strange for me. The first couple years of my popularity, I'd reveled in all the attention from my female fans, enjoying the beauties throwing themselves at me. Living in the all-boys home for seven years, and then going to a college where I'd had no choice but to study every waking second or risk losing my full-ride scholarship, I hadn't had much experience in dating. It wasn't until after I graduated, hosted that first one-off documentary on my school, and then got my own show, *No Trespassing*, when I started letting loose and enjoying the less work-related things in life, like women.

And for the first two years, it had been a steady stream, sometimes a couple different women during each weeklong stay at a location we were shooting. Then the excitement wore off, and the panties being thrown in my direction and the constant flow of vag-pics became more annoying than tantalizing. Not to mention, dealing with the ones who didn't get the concept of a one-night stand—which I always made perfectly clear that's all I had to offer—and became obsessed with me, blasting their stories of our short interactions on the internet, garnering me the reputation of a womanizing Casanova.

So for the last five years, I've mostly avoided sticking my dick anywhere I don't know for certain they'll leave me the fuck alone afterward. The handful of fuck buddies I have spread throughout the continent are enough to take the edge off when I can't take the solitude any longer. And now that I think about it, it's been a good seven months since I even called one of them up. My nightly sessions with my hand had been fueled by what I had thought was an apparition, a dream woman my brain maybe conjured up, a face I might've seen in one of my history books, but who is actually the beautifully wrecked creature who now sits mere inches away from me.

Her eyes meet mine, and I try not to visibly react to what I see in them, what is left of her now-broken spirit. "What are we going to do, Dean?" she asks, and the hopelessness in her voice brings out something inside me, something that makes me want to take away that fear and replace it with the light I'd seen in her when she was dancing around the cavern only a half hour before.

I look her in the eyes, stand, give her my most devastating smile, and hold out my hand to her. "We're going to explore."

Emmy

I HESITANTLY PLACE MY hand in Dean's, allowing him to pull me to my feet, and then place my bag around me with its crossbody strap. I go to reach for my backpack on the ground, but he waves me off, putting his arms through the straps of the bright sequined bag, and I can't help but find him cute. He looks completely unfazed by wearing a hot-pink sparkly backpack, making me draw my lips between my teeth to keep from laughing. That and the chivalry of the act itself is not something I imagined Dean Savageman doing.

Add that to the list of surprises from the man since he scared the living daylights out of me when he first showed up in the cavern. Seeming to act on pure instinct, he'd grabbed me in the nick of time and started hauling ass right before the ceiling of the entrance could collapse on top of us, picking me up and running like I weigh nothing, my heavy-ass bags in tow. Then, when the rubble settled, he didn't yell at me, he didn't call me names or do anything to make me feel worse for my complete stupidity... my childish, idiotic, careless, rooky mistake. When I expected him to add to my pity party, he gave me space until I ran out of tears, then he'd spoken so gently to me that it snapped me out of my never-ending stream of self-deprecation.

And when I asked him what we were going to do, his reply had me flashing back to my bath just a couple hours earlier. I'd asked myself, *What would Dean do?* And as if I was psychic, he'd answered exactly how I imagined.

"We're going to explore."

The words themselves and the way he said them, full of excitement, along with his incredible eyes looking down into mine, I felt my core clench. He was suddenly the Dean from my nightly fantasies, not the one I taught myself to hate.

As much as this should be killing me right now, having to share my catacombs with the normally infuriating man, the one I'd conditioned myself to despise for the past two years, I just don't have it in me. And the way he literally saved my life, I have to admit I'm feeling a little bit fangirlish toward him. Not because of who he is or because of his fame, but because he was like a real life superhero the way he swooped me up and got us out of danger. So when I'd normally be a brat and want to throw a tantrum, I allow myself to grasp onto the pleasant feeling of being in Dean's presence. I even have the thought, *Do you know how many people would* kill *to explore a site with* the *Dean Savageman?*

A lot. Like, a shit load. And seeing how he technically beat me here anyways, I decide to look on the bright side: I am finally fucking realizing my dream. I am inside one of the off-limits places hardly anyone in the world even knows about. I'll be discovering pieces of history right alongside the sexy documentary host.

We'll just ignore the fact I destroyed a huge chunk of it by getting pissed off at a boner.

I follow Dean—and my sparkly backpack—as he starts making his way deeper into the tunnel, and I take a moment to compose myself while he isn't looking. I use my sweater from my purse to wipe the tears and dust from my cheeks as I walk a few feet behind him, and then brush off the dirt from my butt and knees where I'd been cuddled up to the fallen ceiling, praying to the archaeology gods to forgive me for my sins. I was parched and could've really used something to drink—

Wait. My backpack! Thank you, fucking drunk munchies!

"Hey, hold up a sec!" I call out, hustling up to him when he stops and turns toward me. I reach behind him, accidentally brushing my boobs against his arm when I spin him around by the strap of my bag. The sensation of them rubbing against his bulging bicep instantly hardens my nipples, and I feel my face heat as I reach into one of the side pockets to grab one of the Gatorades I'd stashed inside. As I crack open one of the plastic bottles, he faces me once again, and I tell myself to ignore my tingling titties, because it's not like he knows what just happened.

That is, until I look up at him while I take a swig of the electrolyte-filled liquid, nearly choking as I guzzle when I see his eyes are zoomed in directly on the pointy peaks in question. I look down, and that's when I discover that in my tipsy haste to start my adventure, I'd forgotten to put my bra back on, and my headlights are switched on to high-beam mode.

Completely mortified, I spin away from him, causing the Gatorade to slosh out of the bottle and directly onto the front of my white tank top. The one without a bra underneath. I squeak as the wetness trickles down my cleavage and doesn't stop until it hits my waistband. I look down at myself and, sure enough, nothing is left to the imagination. The only thing that keeps me from screaming to force another boulder to fall and smoosh me right there is the fact I grabbed the white flavor as apposed to the red one, so at least I don't look like I've been shot. With a curse, I throw off my purse and pull on my jacket, zipping it up to my throat. Yes, I'll end up sweating like pig in no time, but at least the ladies will be hidden from the smoldering gaze I see coming from Dean as I finally turn back to face him.

He finally tears his eyes away from my chest to look into my embarrassed face, and tries his best to keep from showing his amusement. I can tell by the twitch of his lips, before he asks, "Are you always this accident prone, or is today just my lucky day?"

"Always. Without failure," I admit easily, because there's no point in lying. I'm a grade-A klutz. Rolling the sleeves of my jacket up, putting my purse strap back over my head, I cringe at the stickiness between my tits.

Seeing my discomfort, Dean says, "You know, I could think of a way to clean up the mess you just made… but I'm pretty sure it would make a new one somewhere else."

My jaw falls open at his ballsy flirtation, and I feel my cheeks grow blazing hot at the image he just placed in my head. My mouth closes and opens like a fish a few times as my eyes go wide. I can't even respond. I am so not used to men coming on to me… especially not ones who look like Dean Savageman.

"Wow, that's all I had to do to get you to quit yelling at me before?" He gives me a mischievous grin, pulls the bottle out of my hand, and proceeds to take a drink, all while I just stare up at him. He slides the Gatorade back into the pocket, turns, and continues on as if he didn't just strike me stupid. I follow dumbly, a quick-witted comeback never finding its way from my brain to my mouth.

Case-in-point, the reason I've never gotten laid outside of losing my V-card my first year of college. The first time I had sex had been the last. It had been awful, awkward, and embarrassing—like most things in my life—and instead of learning to hone my womanly skills, I'd focused on my studies, basically retarding my social skills by locking myself away and immersing myself in all things historical. I often told myself it was okay that I lived vicariously through my ho of a best friend, Erin, but according to the one time I let her shrink that part of my personality, she told me it was post-traumatic stress from losing my virginity that caused me to never have the guts to try it again. She also said the only way I'd ever get over it was to "Suck it up, buttercup. You'll never get over it unless you save a horse and ride a different cowboy." That was the last time I asked her for advice while we were at a country bar.

I usually put off a please-don't-talk-to-me vibe when we go out, and knowing how uncomfortable male attention makes me, or any attention for that matter, Erin usually pretends to be my lesbian lover to help me avoid having to interact with anyone of the opposite sex. It's no wonder using my feminine wiles didn't get me into any sites, 'cause lord knows I haven't had any practice.

Now that I think about it, besides Ricky and Calvin, I've exchanged more words with Dean than any other man in… well, ever, that didn't consist of me begging to get into a site. And even more alarming, I have never, in all the times I've run into him across the country, been nervous around him. My hatred toward him far outweighed my awkwardness, so I never had to deal with a panic attack or not knowing what to say, just because of the equipment he had between his legs.

I mean, I know I'm not ugly. Both my parents are ridiculously good-looking people. But my inside doesn't seem to match up with my outside. If you were able to project what I looked like internally onto a wall, you'd see a slight girl with mousy brown hair, thick glasses, a full mouth of braces, a flat chest covered by a button up shirt and a plaid jumper, sitting at a desk covered in history books while listening to the movie score of the *Avengers* as she studied, not for school but for pleasure.

It was superheroes, voodoo shops, and museums that made my soul happy. Not makeup, boys, and… whatever else most girls were into. I'd managed to find the one other girl in elementary school who loved learning as much as I did, and we've been inseparable ever since. Erin was as big into psychology as I was archaeology, even when we were kids. Since we had each other, we never really had to worry about what other people thought of us. And because we locked ourselves away in our "Nerd Cave" as Dad teasingly called it, our bodies might've changed on the outside as we grew up, but our love of all things geeky never did.

We often go to Comic-Cons, where I dress up as Rocket Raccoon from *Guardians of the Galaxy* and Erin as Khaleesi from *Game of Thrones*, excited to hang out with like-minded people. It's the only time I can really tolerate being in a crowd. I think it's because I'm able to hide behind my costume. Yet, for some reason, everyone is always surprised when we jump into conversations, throwing in our own theories of what will happen in the next season of *Stranger Things*, or who Jon Snow's parents *really* are.

But in Erin's case, since she's always had such an outgoing personality and not a single awkward bone in her body, she's never had a problem with the opposite sex. Plus, being a psychologist, she can read people shockingly clear upon first meeting them, and knows how to get what she wants out of them. It's a good thing she's such a good person, because it's scary to think what she'd be able to do with that 'superpower' of hers, as we call it.

"Check this out," Dean says, and I almost run into the back of him, not paying attention during my mental ramblings.

"What is it?" I ask, squinting in the direction in which he points. I pull my phone out of my purse and turn on the flashlight app, shining it on the wall of the tunnel, still seeing nothing. Dean places his hands around mine, sending another jolt of electricity up my arms as he aims the beam of light at a tiny placard the same color as the wall, the single word chiseled into it.

"*Trois*," he reads aloud. "French for three." He looks down at me with a curious look on his face.

"Well, there are three tunnels that come off the cavern. Counter-clockwise, this would be the third tunnel. Maybe they labeled them to keep it stupid-proof." I shrug.

"Could be," he agrees, but he doesn't seem convinced. I want to just blow it off and continue our exploration, but knowing he has years more of experience than me, I decide it would be wise to take note. He pulls out his own phone and snaps a picture of the placard.

"What are you thinking?" I question, looking more closely at the sign to see if there might be something on it he sees that I don't.

"Well, I went down one of the other tunnels, and there wasn't a sign in there except for the one telling all the different dates in which the bones had been emptied from somewhere else and stacked down here. I just find it odd is all," he explains, but then seems to shrug it off and continues walking. We don't make it much farther before he stops once again, this time shining his flashlight app on a placard on the wall, just above the ground. "*Deux*. Why would there be a marking for two?" he mumbles to himself. Then he looks to me, and adds, "Well, I guess we know it's not a sign numbering the tunnels." He snaps a picture of this one then keeps walking.

As we traverse the seemingly never-ending channel, I search the walls, floor, and ceiling, trying to spot the tiniest things out of place. Dean spotted those camouflaged markers so easily, when I would have walked right past them. I find myself starting to become more and more in awe of the man than jealous. I could learn so much from him if I could put aside the negative feelings of the past.

Finally, I spot something as he walks right beneath it. I stop and stare upward, but I am too short to read it clearly. "Here!" I call out, and he hurries back to where I stand, shining my phone's light up at the ceiling. "I can't make it out, can you?" I watch him squint and can't help admiring the strong angle of his jawline as he tries to see what the marker says. I quickly look away when his gaze falls to me and he sees I was staring at him and not the placard. "I can't see it either. Hmm… oh, wait." He pulls out his cell and I watch as he brings up his camera, using two fingers on the screen to zoom in on the ceiling, but the image is too blurry to read.

"Damn it," I curse, and before I can think better of what I'm doing, or where the balls come from that I suddenly grow, I take off my purse and set it on the ground, then reach for my backpack on Dean's shoulders.

"What are you doing?" he asks, but allows me to slide the bag off his arms and put it next to my purse.

"Stoop down. I'm going up," I say, and with a surprised look that turns into a grin, he takes me by the shoulders, spins me away from him, uses one of his booted feet to kick mine apart, and I let out a squeal when suddenly his head comes out from between my legs and he stands up. It happens so fast my world spins, but I feel his strong hands grip my thighs at the same time my hands wrap under his chin.

"Can't breathe, love," he squeezes out, and I feel the words vibrate against my palms where they hold on to his throat.

Me neither, I think, as all my attention focuses directly where my core rests against the back of his neck. I feel the heat of his body seep into mine through my jeans, and I pull my lips between my teeth. *Dear Lord, I know you have a great sense of humor, usually at my expense, but just this one time, please… please, help a sistah out and don't let me soak the man's neck. No wetty right now, okay? Pretty please?*

"Emmy," he wheezes, and it snaps me out of my silent prayer.

"I'm sorry! You just took me by surprise. I went from 5'6" to well over eight feet high," I apologize, loosening my grip around his throat.

"Can you see it now?" he asks, lifting his chin to look upward, and all that does is rub the back of his head against my lady bits, causing a wave of tingles to run from my clit down to the tips of my toes.

I unconsciously let out a moan and I have to fight myself not to grind my hips. The sound startles me, and I jump, slapping my hand over my own mouth. *Oh, God. Please, don't let him have heard that.*

"Emmy?" His voice is low and husky, and I cringe at what he might say next.

"Yeah, Dean?" I whimper.

"Can… can you see the sign?"

I can tell by his stutter he wanted to say something else, but had mercy on me instead. I let out a sigh of relief and look up. I can make out that the word has three letters, but it's still too blurry to read what it says. "Still a little too far away. Hand me your phone," I tell him, and I feel his right hand leave my thigh as he reaches into his pocket then up to hand me his cell. I flip on the camera and snap a picture with the flash on then pull up the photo and zoom in. "I got it! It says *six*," I say excitedly, unintentionally wiggling on top of his shoulders, sending yet another burst of electricity throughout my body. This time, I'm able to stifle my moan by biting my lip, and when I feel like I can speak again, it's to say, "Okay, you can let me down now."

He smoothly lowers us until my feet touch the ground and he comes out from underneath me, and I immediately miss the heat of him against my core. That is, until I see him reach up to rub the back of his neck like he's wiping something off, which sends me into a mortification that has me crying out, "It's sweat, I swear!"

This time, when he tries to hold in his amusement, he fails, and he lets out a chuckle that raises the hair on my arms it's so gloriously sexy. Almost worth my humiliation to hear that sound come out of him. "No worries, love. Just had a little crick in my neck from lying around in the other tunnel earlier."

"Oh, umm... so, yeah." I clear my throat. "So now we have, three, two, and six. Um, shall we keep looking?" I ask, and to my ears it sounds more like a plea. What I wouldn't give for the tunnel floor to open up and swallow me.

A few minutes later, we find yet another sign, but this one is set into the floor and is written out in numerals. *1618.*

"Is it a date?" I wonder aloud. "Three, two, six, 1618. March 26th, 1618?"

"Maybe, or a couple of other dates if we scrambled up the numbers. But that wouldn't make any sense down here. New Orleans wasn't even founded until exactly a hundred years later, in 1718," Dean says.

"And the NOLA catacombs didn't start being built until St. Peter Cemetery filled up in the 1780s," I add. A feeling close to pride fills my chest when he looks at me with an impressed expression. *Yeah, big guy. I know my shit.* "So what else could it be?"

"All sorts of things, but maybe we should keep searching. See if there are any more markers before we go trying to play Word Scramble without having all the missing letters first," he suggests smartly.

I nod in agreement, wiping sweaty strands of hair from my face. The deeper into the tunnels we've traversed, the hotter and muggier it seems to be getting, and before long, I can't take it anymore. We've walked for ten minutes scouring every inch of the walls without finding another placard. My shirt would probably be dry by now from the Gatorade incident if I wasn't sweating under my jacket, and if I don't take it off, I'm going to pass out from heat exhaustion.

Note to self: start working out to build endurance if I'm going to be doing this the rest of my life.

As soon as I even think about the fact I'm not wearing a bra under my white tank top as I unzip the front of my jacket, my nipples perk up as if I whistled for their attention. Yet survival outweighs embarrassment, so off my jacket comes, and I wrap it in its normal spot around the strap of my purse.

Just act natural, I chant to myself, but that thought flies out the window when I look up and find Dean's eyes locked on my chest.

My breath catches as he walks slowly toward me, towering above me when he finally stops mere inches away. My heart gives one wild thump as he lifts his hand, and I think he's going to have the audacity to grab my boob, but he traces my collarbone instead.

"The Atlantis Ring," he mumbles, as his finger glides across my skin, sending goose bumps downward and tightening my nipples further.

"Known previously as the Ring of Luxor," I manage to squeak, knowing his gaze is following the lines of the small tattoo on my left collarbone. Suddenly, he pulls his hand away and unzips his hoodie, and I immediately start to panic. What is he doing? Why is he stripping? Do I need to make a run for it? It's not like I have anywhere to go. I'm trapped in here if all of a sudden my tattoo has mystical Egyptian powers I didn't know about that hypnotized him and he's now about to ravish me without my consent.

But really, would it be without your consent, Em?

The teeniest part of me still wants to hang onto my old feelings of contempt toward Dean, but after actually being around him, speaking to him, being on this adventure with him, the rest of me tells that small part to shut the hell up. The real him, not the cocky know-it-all everyone sees on the show, is pretty damn amazing.

He pulls off his sweater, revealing nothing but a thin, ribbed black tank top underneath, and it makes me realize I've never actually seen his arms before. Not even on the show. He always wears the same outfit every episode: a dark pair of jeans and his signature dark grey hoodie with a brown pair of hiking boots. What stands before me is a man with the sexiest pair of arms I've ever seen in my life. Straight up arm porn. The biceps are huge and the forearms sinewy, corded with muscles I've never seen outside a fitness magazine.

And wrapped around one of those delicious forearms is the Ring of Luxor, just a much larger version than the one on my collarbone.

SIX

DEAN

OF ALL THE COUNTLESS SYMBOLS in the entire world we could tattoo permanently into our skin, what are the odds that Emmy and I would choose the exact same one? The Atlantis Ring, aka the Atlantean Ring, and yes, the beautiful, brilliant girl was exactly right, also historically known as the Ring of Luxor when it was first discovered by the French Egyptologist Marquis d'Agrain around 1860 in a tomb in the Valley of the Kings.

She reaches toward me with one hand and traces her middle three fingers along the three main long rectangular lines in the center of the six black squares, all bracketed by two large triangles. When she speaks, her words come out hushed but clear.

"My parents have had this symbol all over our house since I can remember. They live in Egypt now, but seeing this in every room of our house since I was little, it's always been a comfort, making me feel at home no matter where I am. That's why I had it tattooed on me—the symbol for protection. I hate crowds, and have anxiety issues. As accident prone as I am, I guess it works after all." She looks up at me and smiles gently. "I could've really gotten hurt back there, if not killed. I was making all sorts of racket, dancing around and singing before I even knew you were down here. That ceiling could've come down any time. If it weren't for you saving me…"

Her words trail off and she looks away, her cheeks glowing an attractive pink. I love the sound of her voice, whether it's throwing angry words at me or making gentle confessions, and I want to hear more of it, so I tell her something I've never told anyone before. "The Atlantean Ring is for protection, yes, but it's also for healing and intuition. I got this tattooed on me after my first episode of the show, the one that didn't end up being aired because of my fuck-up."

She looks up at me, curiosity filling her beautiful green eyes. "I was doing an episode on bridges around the US. We were on day three of filming, on an old bridge in Kentucky they were refurbishing, and I thought I would be a hot shot and walk across one of the beams while I recited my lines. There was no one there besides me and my cameraman, since we'd gotten there early to rehearse first, and little did I know that the beam I chose to use as a catwalk was one that hadn't been secured yet. My weight on it was just enough to make one of the ends come off its ledge where it was balanced. As the beam plummeted a hundred feet to the rocks below, by the grace of God, I managed to grab onto the ledge, and then with my cameraman's help, I was pulled to safety."

"Oh, my God," she breathes, and I have to wonder if she realizes she's grasped my arm, her little hand searing my flesh.

"I got this tattooed soon after. In a book I read about it, it said, 'The one who wears the ring becomes sensitive to certain communications that he would never have been aware of. It increases one's intuition and ability to connect with higher levels of consciousness and Spirit guides.' I just really liked the thought of that, like putting a magic spell on myself that would let me *talk to dead people*," I whisper the last part and give her a mischievous grin. "I don't know. I guess I just hoped it would make me smarter on my excavations, keep me out of trouble and from doing stupid shit like that again."

"And the healing part?" she asks.

I feel myself wanting to open up to her and tell her all the pain of my past, but I pussy out. "Uh…" I rub the back of my neck with the hand not connected to the arm she's still holding onto. "That's a story for another time, love."

She lets go of me and rubs her palm up and down her thigh. "Oh, um, sorry. That was kinda nosey of me, huh? Well, uh… yeah. So. Should we look for more markers?" She pulls her hair down from her messy ponytail and uses both hands to smooth her damp tendrils out of her flawless face, tying it back up into a knot on top of her head. The act is unintentionally sexy as hell, as it lifts her breasts high against the white cotton of her thin tank top and shows off the feminine line of her graceful neck.

"Yeah. There's gotta be something else here that will shed more light on what we've found so far," I agree, and open up her shiny-ass backpack to stuff my hoodie inside, when I see it's full of enough junk food to feed a small country. I glance back up to her with a raised brow, and she has the most adorable sheepish look on her face.

"Well, uh… you see, what happened was…" She starts to giggle nervously. "Ugh! Okay, I was super pissed off at you for thwarting yet another one of my discoveries—"

"Thwarting?" I interrupt with an amused smirk.

"Yes, *thwarting*. To thwart, or spoil, or in your case *steal* my goddamn glory," she huffs, but thankfully, I can see she's fighting her own smile, as opposed to being genuinely angry with me like before. She crosses her arms, pressing those amazing tits of hers together, as she continues with her story. "So I went to my pub and shot back fifteen dollars' worth of three-dollar tequila shots. Then, I was chatting with Calvin and Ricky in my bathtub and—"

Instantly, an unfamiliar boiling rage fills me, and I cut her off once more. "You were with two men in your bathtub?" I growl, the thought filling me with a possessiveness I've never felt toward a woman before.

"Huh? Oh—*No!* Calvin and Ricky are *married*. And we were Snapchatting. They live in like, Ohio or something." Her cheeks flame red, and it settles the beast that snarled inside me. "*Anyways,* the combination of Patron in my system and them telling me I needed to break out the big guns, which in my case was doing something illegal for the first time in my life, I jumped out of the tub, threw on my clothes, and ran out the door to come sneak in, stopping only long enough to grab some food for my drunk munchies. You were supposed to be gone!" she whines.

I shake my head and grin. "And if I had been gone as planned, how exactly had you intended on breaking in?" I inquire, reaching down to adjust my cock, stiffening at her haughtiness.

"I came armed with a bobby pin and a credit card, thank you very much." A pause. "And why the hell do you keep doing that?" she asks, waving her hand in the direction of my now fully inflated dick, exasperation lacing her voice.

"I can't help it, love. Something about you yelling at me just does something to me. I guess I'm just not used to anyone in the female population giving me shit," I tease. But her response isn't what I expect out of a sexy-as-fuck woman such as her. Instead of coming back at me for the cocky comment about my vast choice of women, she looks almost mortified.

"Oh, I uh… I didn't know men…" She trails off, but what she

did sputter intrigues me.

"Surely you know your hot little temper is sexy as hell, love," I prompt, raising an eyebrow.

"Um… so…" She fidgets with the strap of her purse, untying and retying her jacket. "Shall we?" she squeaks, and hurries past me deeper into the tunnel.

I chase after her, getting in front of her, and turn to walk backward so I can look at her while I press further. "Finish your sentence, Emmy. You didn't know men what?"

She tries to dodge around me, not meeting my eyes, but I duck in front of her once more, stooping down to hold her shifty gaze. "You should know, I don't give up when I want something. So you might as well go ahead and give in so we can continue on our little adventure." I stop abruptly, and she crashes into me, just as I'd hoped. Her softness molds to my front for a moment before she bounces back, and I reach out and grab hold of her hips to keep her from falling on her ass.

God, just that split second of full-frontal contact, and my cock throbs behind my zipper. My hands burn into her hips through her jeans, and all I want to do is tear through her clothes and have my way with her, right here on the catacombs' ground. The closeness must have an affect on her as well, because her eyes are no longer darting away, but gazing deep into mine, the green orbs seeming to stare straight into my very soul, making me hold my breath to hear what she might say. What started as joking curiosity has now turned into a dire need for her answer.

"I… I didn't know men could get turned on so easily, and at something I did unintentionally," she admits quietly.

My eyebrows pull together. Such an innocent and honest statement from a woman who looks like she could eat her fill of men for breakfast. Something so innocuous could only come from someone who doesn't have much experience with the subject in question. But certainly… no. No way. Not with a body that would be a siren's call to any man within a mile, and the face of an angel, prompting even the most closed-off male to want to open up to her. Not to mention a brain that would give the most intellectual guy a boner at the thought of mentally sparring with her in between fucking her on every surface within reach.

The thought of *any* man fucking her on *any* surface causes the beast inside me to snarl once again, and my hands unconsciously squeeze her full hips, pulling her closer to me. But then it also has me questioning my original thought. How innocent is Amelia…? Jesus, I don't even know her last name. How can I feel this possessive over a woman, when I don't even know her full name? Just that she's named after her mother's hero, that we have matching tattoos—one she couldn't have seen on my show and copied, because I purposely never showed it on camera, not wanting anyone to know even the smallest personal detail—and that she has more of an effect on me than any other woman in my twenty-nine years.

This close to her, with her looking up at me with those eyes, her innocence glaringly clear in their depths, it all makes sense. She's the female version of me. Headstrong toward one thing—her love of archeology—she probably hadn't spent any time worrying about the opposite sex, focusing on her education so she could live out her dream, the same as I did. Only she's just starting out on her journey, and obviously hadn't gotten the big break I had.

Feeling her kindred spirit, I have the fleeting thought that maybe my Atlantean Ring tattoo's intuition property is working its magic, because I feel like I can see right down into this beautiful woman's pure soul. And with that thought, I lower my head and capture her perfect, pouty lips with mine, feeling her stiffen slightly before melting against me. In that kiss, with her shuttered breaths and tentative movements, her hands lightly pressing to my cotton-covered stomach, I just know she doesn't have much, if any, experience with being intimate, so I happily yet gently take the lead.

One of my hands travels up her back and cradles the back of her head as I take her fully into my arms, holding her close as I mold her front to mine while my mouth dances lazily across hers, teasing it with my lips until she smiles slightly at the ticklish touch. I take advantage and lightly nip her bottom lip before sucking it between mine, running my tongue over the plumpest part of it. She gasps at the sensation, and I dip my tongue in to tease hers out to play. She doesn't seem to know quite how to move it against mine, so I whisper, "Just do what I do," before running the tip softly down the center of hers, lapping at her mouth until she lets out a whimper. After a few moments' practice, she gets the hang of it, and soon, we're battling for dominance as her control visibly snaps.

SEVEN

Emmy

I'VE KISSED BOYS BEFORE. My first kiss was by a boy dressed as Batman while we were out trick or treating when I was eight and he saw that I was dressed as Catwoman. No clue who the little guy was. He just ran up and gave me a smooch right on my lips before hustling on to the next house for more candy. I can remember our parents giggling with each other after the quick-as-lightning exchange took place more than the actual kiss itself, since it happened out of nowhere and was over before I even knew it began.

Then there was Lance in high school. He was a friend of Erin's and mine who shared our love of history and often studied with us, even when there wasn't a test to be preparing for. He had a crush on Rebecca Barbara Broussard. I can't even think back to her without it being her full name, because that's how she always introduced herself, like some sort of debutante. Anyway, he'd finally scored a date with the sweet southern belle, and was super nervous about the end of the night kiss he was hoping she'd give him. When he asked if he could practice on me, it really wasn't even a big deal. He was my best guy friend and I would do anything to help him out. When we'd kissed, the purely physical act was pleasant enough, and when it ended a few moments later, we went right back to the conversation we'd been having on the history of the Golden Gate Bridge.

Finally, there was Paul, the guy I ended up losing my virginity to. We went on a few dates, more than I'd been on with any other guy to this day, and we shared some kisses at the end of each date. At the end of the first semester during our freshman year, he invited me to a party his frat was throwing. Although crowds, especially rambunctious ones, usually sets off my anxiety, I decided since I'd scored the highest grade in the class that I needed to celebrate, so I agreed to go to my first and only party of my college career.

Erin came with me, and we drank red Solo cups of Jungle Juice—a huge storage tub full to the top with fruit punch, Everclear, grapes, and cherries—before she found one of Paul's fraternity brothers to spend the rest of the evening with, but not before encouraging me to finally lose my V-card. God, it was awful, to say the least. I don't even want to think about it right now.

What I want to think about in this very moment is the best damn kiss I've ever had in my entire life. Never mind the fact it's being given to me by my self-proclaimed mortal enemy, who has now turned into my life-saving hero who fascinates me more and more with every moment I spend with him.

I don't know what to focus on. The feel of his tongue sliding against mine in a rhythmic dance I've never felt before. The most overwhelming yet comforting embrace as his massive arms wrap completely around my much smaller frame. The strong hand at the back of my head that gently guides me into angles that deepen the hottest kiss I've ever experienced. The sexy sound of his breath coming in and out of his nose and mouth just as heatedly as my own, filling the tunnel with the echoes of our earth-shattering exchange.

I didn't know kisses could feel like this. For the rest of my life, this is the one all other kisses will be compared against. And I have a sneaking suspicion none will even hold a candle.

Suddenly, I'm aware I'm moving, and our kiss is broken long enough for Dean to pull my purse over my head and drop it to the ground. The next thing I know, I feel a hard surface at my back as he presses me against the wall, and then I'm weightless as he lifts me, and instinctively my legs wrap around his waist. This puts me at a different angle, slightly higher than him, and not an ounce of uncertainty is present as I use the opportunity to explore his mouth with my tongue.

Subconsciously, I'm aware of the motion of my hips as I grind my center against his abs, not caring I won't be able to pass off the wetness growing there as just sweat. If he can be completely shameless about the rock-hard bulge in his pants, then by God, I can embrace this amazing, freeing feeling I have as I cling to him and put my very soul into this kiss.

Yet the second I feel his hand on the skin of my side as he reaches beneath my tank, the escalation from first to second base is as shocking as if a stadium full of fans exploded into cheers, and I jerk my head back. If it weren't for his hand still tangled in the back of my hair, I would've cracked my head on the wall.

I stare down into his eyes, embarrassment at my reaction starting to fill me. But instead of finding confusion or disappointment in his face, I find understanding, as if I just confirmed something he'd been pondering, and it lessens my shame.

"Damn, love. You are one hell of a kisser. And I suspect a fast learner too. Am I right?" he asks quietly, and then leans forward to kiss the tattoo on my collarbone, sending shivers throughout my body.

"Apparently," I breathe, relaxing once more into his embrace.

"Have you never been kissed before?" His voice is gentle, as if trying not to make a big deal about it so he doesn't scare me away. It works.

"Not like that," I admit.

He continues his trail of kisses up my chest and across my throat until he reaches my ear, where he asks in a whisper, "Have you never been with anyone before?"

I stiffen a little, my legs clenching around his waist, but I've been more open with him than even the guy I lost my virginity to, so why stop now? "Once, a long time ago."

He pulls his head away to look into my eyes, his eyebrows slightly pulled together. "Just the once?"

"Um, yeah," I confess. "It was terrible, and I never felt the desire for a repeat experience. If that's what sex was supposed to be like, then it was something I could live without. I found my studies much more satisfying."

"I actually get that," he says, surprising me. "It's been quite a while for me too. And I have to tell you, I've never felt a kiss like that before."

I feel my cheeks heat, but this time, it's not from embarrassment. His words make me feel better about my weird quirks than anyone has since my best friend and parents. I've always felt a bit ashamed that my brain doesn't focus on the same stuff other girls do, like there was something wrong with me for never being boy crazy or having even the slightest yearning for anything but fulfilling my dream of being an archaeologist. I've always had a one-track mind, never veering off course or letting anything distract me from my goals. It's always just been me trying to progress, my sights set on my one purpose, and it dawns on me that my legs are currently wrapped around my biggest roadblock for the past two years.

The thought makes me snort, and amusement fills his now dark blue eyes, so smoldering that I can barely make out the gold flecks I know are there. "What?" he prompts.

I wiggle a little, indicating I want down, and he reluctantly lets me slide down his body until my feet hit the ground. "I just realized I had a make-out session with the one guy who's been standing in the way of everything I've worked for since I was young. And you know what? I'm not even mad about it."

He quirks his head at me, studying my face like he's trying to figure out what's going on in my brain. "Funny thing is, love, at all those places I saw you, I honest to God thought you were a ghost I'd picked up on one of my excavations. If you'd spoken to me…" He shakes his head. "There's no way I would've turned down such a beautiful, intelligent woman as yourself, if you'd asked to check out one of the locations with me. I would've let you tag along in a heartbeat."

My mouth falls open. I don't know whether to laugh, scream, cry, or what. All I know is my chest tightens and I want to throw the hissy fit to end all hissy fits. Gah! Two years. Two *fucking* years I've held onto these ugly feelings toward a man who not only saved my life, but come to find out would've opened up and held the door to let me step right into my dream. So many times I'd written out hate mail to send to the man I'd been completely jealous of, always deleting it, thinking it would've never reached him anyways. When all I had to do was ask him the first time I'd seen him if I could come with him.

I'm trembling with my fury at myself, but I at least have the mind to not scream out my frustration and bring the ceiling down on our heads… again. I take a few deep breaths, trying to calm my nerves, and I feel some of my anger leave me when he lifts my chin to meet his eyes.

"Little did I know you weren't an apparition, but a real life angel here on earth," he tells me, and I feel my lip tremble. God, I'm such a horrible human being. How could I have judged him so terribly?

"You wouldn't be saying that if you knew the awful things I've said about you in the last couple years," I confess, but instead of looking hurt that someone he didn't even know had been talking shit about him, he looks amused and even chuckles a little.

"And I'm sure I deserved every single name you called me, just not for the reason you said them," he pledges. He takes a step back, a smile still on his face, and he bends down to pick up my bags. "As much as I would love to continue what we started, I don't want to risk scaring you away when I just found you. How about… we forget about the recent past, and focus more on the one from centuries ago? Because I don't know about you, love, but I am dying to know what these bread crumbs could be leading us to."

Wow, there's so much in what he said that I could pick apart and analyze—especially that guilt-healing part about not wanting to scare me away when he just found me—but what I gather as a whole is that he forgives me for all my previous malevolence and wants to keep exploring where this adventure could take us.

DEAN

SHE'S A GODDAMN UNICORN. I fucking knew it! Thank you, Atlantean Ring. This gorgeous, smart-as-hell, voracious, and goal-driven creature has had sex only once in her life? Really? I mean, the thought of any man having his hands on her, even once, makes me want to find him and choke him out, which I try not to focus on at the moment, because shit, it could be worse. Much worse. I could've been forced to crave a woman who'd had countless sexual partners in the past that I would have to fume about. So I can live with just the one. And only the one time, she said. And it was so terrible she didn't even want to talk about it.

I would pull the information out of her later, but after her reaction to my fingers touching the softest skin I've ever felt when I got a little handsy during our make-out session, I decide not to push her too far too soon. The ferocious feline I thought she was in the beginning is actually more of a skittish kitten, and I don't want to do anything to frighten her away when I really want to pet her. Even if it is fun to watch her claws come out.

We walk slowly down the tunnel, searching carefully for any more clues to our mystery, and right when I'm about to get discouraged, thinking there isn't anything left for us to find, Emmy squeals from my right, "Got one, Dean!"

I hurry over, my cell already out to shine light and take a picture, seeing this one reads *Nombre d'Or*. I know *nombre* means 'number' in French, but I'm not sure of the rest. It's right there on the cusp of my brain. Something familiar. Something that wants to click into place. I know this. Why won't it reveal itself to me?

"The Golden Ratio," she breathes, and there it is. "The Golden Ratio, Dean!" She jumps up, running in place and waving her hands out in front of her. "It all makes sense! 1618. One-point-six-one-eight! It's the fucking Golden Ratio!"

Like a bucket of ice water being dumped over my head, everything falls into place. And I jump up and start dancing around with her, feeling like a kid again—better, actually—when all the numbers we've found start aligning themselves in my brain with perfect clarity.

Like a nerd version of a dance crew, I freeze into a robot pose, while she does the running man and names off a fact about the Golden Ratio. "Sacred Geometry, universal patterns used in the design of virtually every-damn-thing in our reality. It can be seen in architecture and art, and is also found in nature. Sacred geometry and math ratios, harmonics, and proportion can also be found in music, light, and cosmology. Go!" She freezes in a pose pointing at me, and I take it as my cue to throw out my own fun fact while making my robot body move.

"Also known as 'God's blueprint', the ratio is all throughout nature. The chambered nautilus grows at a continuous rate, so its shell forms a logarithmic spiral to accommodate that growth without changing its shape. Just like honeybees construct hexagonal compartments to hold their honey. Go!"

I point back at her and still, and she hops facing the left, shakes her sexy ass, hops to the back, shakes it again, and continues in a circle, as she sings out, "The Golden Ratio was used to build the Great Pyramid of Giza, the Parthenon, and even the United Nations Building. And it can be found in art like the Mona Lisa and the Statue of Venus. This is why they are so aesthetically pleasing to the human eye. Go!"

I grab my foot behind me in one hand and place my other hand behind my head, and then crunch my knee to my elbow, while calling out, "It's found countless times in flora, but most commonly in the number of petals on a flower. Go!"

When she breaks out the sprinkler, I realize with every fact we yell out to each other that I have never had this much fun with a woman before, and I can feel myself falling for her, which is crazy. I've known her all of a couple hours, even though I had unknowingly been coming to her perfect face for years.

"The Golden Ratio in the human body. Ready?" she asks, starting to pant with all the exertion of our sweet dance battle.

I nod and grin, crossing my arms over my chest like I'm getting ready for her to deliver her side of the fight. "Challenge accepted."

"The bones in your fingers," she wheezes, as she attempts to twerk, but fails miserably.

My turn. "Length between your shoulder line, and the length of your head."

She stops dancing, trying to catch her breath, but still says, "Length between fingertip to elbow, and length between your wrist and elbow.

I keep my feet still, but move my arms to dance the shopping cart, as I name, "Width of your adorable nose, and length between its nostrils." That makes her smile shyly, and she pushes some of her fallen hair out of her face with the back of her hand. I stop dancing and saunter up to her, my cock already hard just from the brilliance of my beautiful Emmy's mind.

Her green eyes look up into mine almost dreamily, and she breathes, "The length between your pupils, and the length between your eyebrows."

"The length of your angelic face, and the width of it," I add, my voice dropping low as I trace a finger along her delicate jawline. Then I cup her jaw and run my thumb over her perfect lips, while whispering, "The width of your delicious mouth, and the width of your nose." I lean down to run the tip of my nose down the bridge of hers before sealing her lips to mine, reveling in the feel of her shuddering breath followed by a sigh of pleasure.

As I pull back to look down at her, her eyes stay closed and I see her visibly swallow. I skip her turn again when she doesn't speak. "Length between your bellybutton to your knee, and the length between your knee and foot." I reach between us to circle her bellybutton through her shirt before sliding my hand downward, running my palm over the firm line of her thigh to her knee before moving inward. I take her mouth in a searing kiss as

I run it up the inseam of her jeans, feeling her jump slightly when I finally reach the top and briskly let my fingers glide over her center, just long enough to feel she is as wet as I am hard.

When I break our kiss once more, her eyes flutter open, and we stare into each other's eyes for what feels like forever, waiting to see what the other will do, until finally she smiles softly, and says, "You win."

For a moment, I think she's giving me permission to let go of the control I have over my raging hunger for her, but just in time, I realize she's talking about our fun fact dance battle. Surprising me, she leans up on her tiptoes and places a sweet kiss to my lips before pulling away and bending down to pick my cell off the ground. She goes to my photos and starts flipping through all the placards while I stand dumbfounded. Jesus, I can barely think straight around this girl.

"Okay, now we know 1618 is really the *Nombre d'Or*, the Golden Ratio, one-point-six-one-eight. So now we need to figure out what the three, two, and six mean," she thinks out loud, and I watch as she crosses one ankle over the other before sliding to the ground to sit Indian-style. How someone so sexy can also look adorably innocent is beyond me, but she does it. I hear her mumbling under her breath, and realize she's saying the clues over and over, each time in a different order, trying to make sense of the sequence. And just when I'm about to tell her we should keep looking, the brilliant woman stiffens, and by the look on her face, I can see she just figured it out.

Her head jerks in my direction as she looks at me, and then her eyes glaze over, as if she's looking straight through me. "One-point-six-one-eight. The Golden Ratio. Three. Six. Two. Three lines. Framed by six squares. Bracketed by two triangles. Dean, the answer is the Atlantean Ring!"

Suddenly, my world spins and my knees give out, and I plop

down onto the ground next to her, reciting part of the book I'd read about the subject so many times I had it memorized like the script to one of my shows. "*The Atlantis Ring's composition follows the Sacred Geometry principles of the Golden Ratio for the alignment of its design elements, proportions, and angles. This design, when properly crafted, will work like an antenna, receiving and transmitting powerful waves that help transmute harmful energies. When you are in this vibration, your energy will merge with the ring's, creating a strong and powerful subtle energy field that will manifest as Protection, Intuition, and Healing.*"

When she says nothing else, I glance in her direction, and see one side of her mouth is lifted in a half smile. When I raise an eyebrow in question, she asks, "Do you memorize everything you read verbatim?"

"Most of the time, yes. Came in handy for college, and even more so now, when I have to learn a ton of information quickly for each new episode," I reply.

We sit for a while in silence, both of us turning the answer over in our brains, yet not understanding what the puzzle was in the first place, until finally she speaks again. "Well what the hell does it all mean?" She jumps to her feet and starts pacing. "Great, we figured out what the numbers mean, and how it all leads to the Atlantean Ring, but—"

"That's it!" I say, hopping up as well.

"What's it?" She stops and looks at me questioningly.

"Say that again. Exactly how you said it before," I tell her excitedly.

"Great, we figured out what the numbers mean, and how it all leads to the Atlantean Ring—"

"Right there! Stop. It all leads to the Atlantean Ring," I repeat, my heart starting to pound.

"That's what I just said. We know what it adds up to, Dean,

but why are all these clues scattered around here, in the NOLA Catacombs?"

"No, love. Think of it more literally. Not the Atlantean Ring, as in the symbol. But the actual..."

"Atlantean Ring," we say in unison, and at the same time I feel a chill roll up my spine and the hairs on the back of my neck stand on end, I see her shiver and rub her arms.

EIGHT

Emmy

"HOLY SHIT!" I EXCLAIM. "But how? Why would the Ring of Luxor be here, in New Orleans, in a place that has been abandoned for over a century?"

"Abandoned, or ingeniously guarded? So well secured that everyone just plain forgot about it?" he offers.

My head is spinning as my mind tries to make sense of everything. When I get overwhelmed like this, I have to talk about it out loud, or I'll make myself crazy. "Okay… okay, Em, think. History. The history of the ring. Mom and Dad used to tell you this shit as bedtime stories, so think. All right. The ring was discovered around 1860 in a tomb in the Valley of the Kings in Egypt by French Egyptologist Marquis d'Agrain. The original ring was made of clay from Assuan, now known as Aswan, a city in southern Egypt that sits on the Nile River. When it was found, it was already ancient, and it is widely believed it was made by the people of Atlantis, Egyptians' predecessors."

Dean picks up where I leave off, when I try to think of where it went after the Frenchman. "It was inherited by his granddaughter, who married a Spaniard by the name of André de Belizal, who was the pioneer of Radiesthesia. I'm not well read in that area, but from what I understand, someone who practices it claims they are extra sensitive to things around them, like the presence of underground water, or they can detect an illness, or even figure out if someone is guilty of a crime. This is usually aided by a pendulum or a divining rod."

I snap my fingers. "Yes! That guy. My mom has one of those pendulums. She used to use it on Dad, but he'd just pretend he was hypnotized and then start clucking around like a chicken." Dean barks out a laugh, the random story catching him off guard. "Sorry." I giggle. "Okay, so the granddaughter and her hubs had it next, but then what?"

"Well, from stories Marquis told him, and from ones told to them by the few people Marquis let wear the ring, it was discovered there seemed to be mysterious powers surrounding it. An entire family getting sick, but the one who wore it staying perfectly healthy. A freak accident, but the one wearing it not suffering a scratch on them. So ole André studied the waves emitted by the ring—which he called the Waves of Luxor—using his radiesthesia, and he figured out that it wasn't the ring itself, but the pattern engraved on it—our tattoo—is what gave it its mystical power of protection."

I spring into the air, remembering my favorite story about the symbol, the story that pushed me to get it permanently tattooed into my skin. "Next came Howard Carter! Howard was *convinced* about the protective properties of the ring, when a lot of people thought it was baloney... just a bunch of hocus pocus, if you will."

I smile lightly, and then it stretches into a wide grin when he interjects, "My favorite childhood movie," before I continue.

"So Howard is a British archaeologist who learns about the ring around the year 1900, and when he puts it on, he claims he has a vision that he would discover a wonder the world had never seen. He, along with his partner, Lord Carnarvon, take a huge team down to Egypt, and in 1922, they discover King Tut's tomb! At the entrance of the tomb, there was an ominous inscription that threatened those who dared disturb the Pharaoh's eternal sleep. Did they listen? Of course not. If they don't believe in a ring having mysterious powers, why would they worry about a silly little curse, right?" I hold my hand out, palm facing up, prompting Dean to play along.

"Right. I mean, what kind of gullible idiot believes in a symbol that can emit energy that protects someone from harm? Psh, nonsense," he replies, and gives me a smirk.

I hold up a peace sign. "Within two years, nearly the entire team, almost *twenty people*, including Lord Carnarvon, died from an inexplicable cause. Boom, dead. Out of nowhere. But there was one who survived. The only one who lived a full life until he died of natural causes. Guess who." I hold my hand out again, even though I'm sure he already knows the story.

He puts his hand to his chest, and in a put-on southern accent, he asks, "Oh my, who could it be?" making me giggle.

"Why, our friendly mystical-wave-believing buddy, Howard Carter!" I squeal, and then do a pirouette, and when I face him again, I stomp my landing, throw my arms out wide, and shake my hands in a 'Ta-da!' motion.

"You're forgetting one thing though, love," Dean says, and I stand up straight before looking at him questioningly. "Howard Carter wasn't wearing the original ring. He was wearing a replica he had made, which it is said he never took off for the rest of his life."

"Shit, that's right. So where did the ring go after André and the granddaughter?" I ask.

"Nobody knows. André studied it for years, and wrote several books on it. He was well respected for all his findings, and left an incredible legacy in his invention of instruments, the pendulums and such, and then documented experiments and research. He and his wife travelled the world with their findings, and come to think of it, I believe I read somewhere that New Orleans was one of her favorite places to visit, seeing how she was of French descent and all," he relays.

"Oh, my God. What if that's it?" I squawk. Now he's the one to give me the confused look. "Dean, there's no way a ring believed to have magical powers just disappeared off the face of the planet. Especially after André did all those experiments that pretty much proved it was real. If it was stolen from him, it would have been recorded *somewhere*. New Orleans was his French-born wifey's favorite vacation spot? Hello! We are in the New Orleans Catacombs, frolicking along a tunnel that has clues spread throughout it that basically spell out 'Altantean Ring This Way!'"

"There was absolutely nothing in the documentation of this site that even mentioned the ring… or even placards on the walls. Usually on maps of these locations, any and all artwork, markings… the tiniest little details, are somehow indicated. Even the most miniscule cracks are specified. It helps with preservation. But here, for the NOLA Catacombs, hardly anything. There was a quickly jotted list of the dates in which cemeteries were emptied and the bones were stacked down here. There was a list of names of famous people who were secretly buried down—"

"Wait, what?" I interrupt, my curiosity getting the best of me.

He smirks and puts me out of my misery. "Only the richest and most infamous of New Orleans' residents knew about the catacombs, because they were the ones who funded it. And they were given the opportunity to reserve plots in one of the tunnels. *Supposedly*, number two is the hoity-toity tunnel, much nicer than this one, number three, which is where the bones of all the emptied cemeteries are if we ever go deep enough. I guess they thought they were too good to be buried amongst the common folk. And then number one was completely empty."

"I find it strange that they started with number three," I think aloud.

He shrugs. "Maybe they were starting at the back and planned on working their way forward."

A thought hits me out of nowhere, and my head whips around as if I've been slapped. "Dean. Let's think of the dates here. The catacombs started being dug out after the cemetery filled up around 1780."

"That's correct," he verifies.

"Let's say it took some time for them to come up with plans for these catacombs, plus the money to do it with…" I prompt.

His eyes look skyward, as if he's searching his brain for the right photographic memory stored there. "If we based it on the technology of the time, and say, compared it to other things that had been built underground around the same time period, these tunnels would have been finished in around eighty years, give or take a decade," he says, confirming my suspicions.

"Exactly eighty years after St. Peter Cemetery filled up in New Orleans, Louisiana, when these catacombs would almost certainly be nearing completion, *French* Egyptologist Marquis d'Agrain discovered the Ring of Luxor in a tomb in the Valley of the Kings in the year 1860. Somewhere between then, and just forty years later, when our good friend Howard Carter tried to get it from André in 1900, it vanished. Poof! Gone. And oh, B-T-Dubs, the last known people to have it just so happened to love coming to

New Orleans, where they were just finishing up a secret, exclusive underground tunnel where only the most infamous and rich people could buy grave plots," I spell out, and I see it in his face when he picks up what I'm throwin' down.

"The perfect place to bury something you never want found."

DEAN

God, this woman is a force to be reckoned with. She figured out the meaning of the numbers. She figured out how the Golden Ratio correlated with the Atlantean Ring. And now, she'd figured out the only reasonable explanation why all this would be here.

I know several people, mostly scholarly type friends of mine, who would chalk all of this up to coincidence. I fall into the fate-believing category. Too much in my life has happened as if it were meant to be, for it all to be coincidence. My mother dropping me off at an orphanage that just so happened to be next to abandoned mines, where I ran away to. The groundskeeper of said orphanage used to work in said mines, and told me stories that would spark a love of history in me that would lead to me focusing all my energy into working my ass off in school. Becoming the first kid from the orphanage and at my Podunk high school to not only receive a full-ride scholarship to college, but to UPenn, the Ivy League school with the best archaeology program in the United States. Being discovered by a TV producer at my job as a tour guide, and then offered my own television show doing what I love.

And it all seems to be leading me to this moment right here. With this enigmatic beauty. God, where did she come from? Where had she been all my life? Well, for the past two, she'd been right there, within arm's reach. The thought I could've been with her this whole time pisses me off a little.

But no, being a believer in fate, I have to believe we weren't supposed to interact until today, when we'd find each other down here in the catacombs, when I could rescue her from being crushed. She would've snuck in either way, finally forcing her way into a site after being rejected so many times. She admitted it herself; that ceiling would've come down whether I was here or not, but I was here to save her on this night.

Then the mutual fascination with the Golden Ratio, her understanding of the French language, I suppose from being from New Orleans, and being able to translate what I couldn't, her parents putting the Atlantean Ring all over their home before moving to Egypt…

Wait. Egypt? Why would a girl's parents leave her here and move all the way to Egypt? Parents who owned pendulums and told their child bedtime stories about King Tut's tomb and French Egyptologists. Who the hell were Emmy's parents?

I look up at her from my still seated position on the ground, and quietly, I ask her, "Hey, love? What's your name?"

She turns her head sideways, probably confused at the abrupt change in subject. "Is that why you keep calling me love? You forgot my name?" She laughs. "Don't feel bad. I never remember people's names the first time they tell me. In one ear and out the other. It's Emmy, short for Amelia—"

I cut her off, "No, no. I remember that. I mean, what's your full name?"

She pulls her hair down out of her knot once more, smoothing all the fallen strands back up into a fresh one, while she replies, "My full name is Amelia Suvan Crain. I told you about the Amelia part, but Suvan is an Egyptian go—"

"Emmy Crain," I interrupt once more, because the realization of who the goddess standing before me is shuts off any manners I might've had to let her ramble adorably. "With parents who own pendulums and use the Atlantean Ring to decorate your home and tell their kid tales of Egyptian history instead of princes and princesses…"

"Well, pharaohs and goddesses," she defends them.

"Your parents are Thomas and Elizabeth Crain. Your parents… are the couple who drove the crawler in the Great Pyramid of Giza. They discovered the queen's chamber!" I explain, as if she doesn't know who her own mom and dad are.

Her mouth falls open and she plops onto her ass, much like I did before, as if the ground had fallen out from under her. "You know my parents?" she prompts, her voice mystified.

"Well, no, I don't like, *know* them. But I know of them! What educated historian and archaeologist wouldn't know the Crains? That husband and wife duo have made *insane* and truly important discoveries," I reply heatedly.

"Right? Oh, my God! You have no idea how many times I've lowered myself to use the whole 'Do you know who I am?' thing while trying to get into sites. Mind you, that was after showing them my dual degree in the subjects. I mean, I didn't go to the fancy schmancy Ivy League school you did, yet mine is nothing to sniff at. But did anyone care? Hell no! Not when they had the rock star of documentaries on their schedule." She crosses her arms and pouts.

There's a lot I could say to all of that, but instead of getting defensive like I would with anyone else, my mind focuses on one minor detail. "You've researched me." Not a question. I've never mentioned on the show or in any post on social media that I went to UPenn. She had to have looked into my background. Not that she would have found much, since I paid a shit load of money to keep my personal life off the internet.

"What? No!" she squawks, and looks away. But it's like the lie immediately eats at her, and she confesses, "Maybe a little."

I scoot closer to her, butting my knees right up against hers while we both sit Indian-style on the dust-covered floor. "So tell me, love. Tell me about myself."

Her cheeks redden, but she doesn't move away. And I feel myself smiling as she names off what little people could find about me on Wikipedia. "You went to UPenn, where you got your degrees in archaeology and history. You worked at the university's museum as a tour guide, before one of The Adventure Channel's producers discovered you and hired you to host UPenn's episode of *Ivy League Schools of America*. Shortly after, you got your own goddamn show, called *No Trespassing*, which is currently in its sixth season and is the top-rated show on The Adventure Channel, and the sixth highest rated show on cable television. You've won three Emmy awards"—I snort, and she glares—"for Outstanding Host for a Reality or Reality-Competition Program. You donate millions to restoration projects. And last time I checked, you have eight scholarship programs with your name on them."

That last part gets my attention. There's no way she found that out with a simple Google search of my name. I try to keep my charity work as quiet as possible, because a lot of it could lead back to personal details I want to keep out of the public eye. The money I donate to reservations, I don't hide, because it would make sense with what people do know about me. But the other...

"How did you find out about the scholarship programs?" I inquire.

"I got on this kick where I wanted to try to make it on my own, without my parents' help. I thought if I let them pay for my education and made it blatantly clear who we were, then I wouldn't be taken seriously as an archaeologist. Everyone would just know me as the Crains' daughter. I wanted to make a name for myself. So I looked into scholarships, and lo and behold, six years ago, when I Googled archaeology financial aid, yours popped up. Back then, you only had one. And I didn't qualify, because I didn't live in foster care." She looks up from her lap and into my eyes. "I wanted to be mad about not being able to apply, but I couldn't. I found it very admirable that you'd want to help those kids out."

Her admission fills me with pride. I was truly lucky where I ended up. I could've been somewhere else, being mistreated or abused. But no. I actually found more love in that orphanage than I ever had before my mother dropped me off. And I feel compelled to tell her about it, which I've never done before. "Mr. Watson," I state.

Her brow furrows. "Pardon?"

"The answer to your question before. Why I call you 'love.' Mr. Watson. He was the groundskeeper of the orphanage I grew up in, and he fell for the lady of the house, our caretaker, Miss Potts. And before you ask, yes, she actually looked just like the *Beauty and the Beast* character—after she became human again, of course—and would sing all the songs to us while she cooked and cleaned. Anyways, he always called her that, simply 'love.' And the way he looked at her… it's like she was the most beautiful thing he'd ever seen. Sort of the way it feels when I look at you." I run a finger along her jawline, watching her intake of breath.

After a moment, I smile at how she decides to respond, obviously too shy to touch on the last part. "You make living in an orphanage sound wonderful," she whispers.

"I mean, there were downfalls. There were some boys who came and went who liked to cause trouble, who were already too messed up by the time they came to live there to realize what we had. And what we had was a loving home with the best mother and father figures we could've ever hoped for, and in my case, a hundred times better than who actually birthed me. They were so extraordinary I never begrudged my mom for leaving me there, because at eleven years old, I was old enough to see and be thankful for what I got handed," I tell her.

"He puked on me," she blurts, and I come out of my reminiscence, feeling more confused than I think I've ever been.

"Wh… what?" I chuckle, shaking my head.

"Sorry, it just came out. I was thinking how amazing it is that you're just opening up and telling me these things about yourself that you've obviously used a lot of energy keeping secret, and then I was thinking how I should share a secret with you, and that's the first thing that flew out of my mouth… kinda like when he puked on me."

"Who? What are you talking about?"

"I told you I had only had sex the one time. In college. And after that, I never did it again because it was so terrible. Well, it was the end of the semester my freshman year, and my best friend and I went to a frat party with the guy I'd been seeing. We drank lots of Jungle Juice, and I finally got it in my head that it was as good a time as any. I didn't have anything to study for. I'd gotten the highest grade in the class, and you grow up being taught that your college years are when you're supposed to get everything out of your system. So, by God, I was going to punch my V-card," she says, and I listen with both curiosity and apprehension.

"So Rin goes off with her flavor of the night, and after a few drinks, Paul took me up to his room. Things were getting hot and heavy—well, what I thought was hot and heavy until… um, you." She blushes and looks to her lap, and her confession helps ease the jealousy I was feeling, as my chest puffs up a bit. "Anyway, well, you see… I didn't tell him I was a virgin."

"Oh no," I mumble, and she shakes her head.

"I know. Lord, don't I know. I didn't want to say anything and risk him not wanting to do it. I wanted my virginity out of the way. It was never anything special to me. I just had never had the desire to do it with anyone. But then the older I got, the more of a burden it felt like, especially with Erin always breathing down my neck about it. It's like my virginity offended her somehow. But anyways. He put on the condom, got on top of me, and I guess just went for it like a guy normally would, thinking a girl was used to having sex."

A feeling of dread creeps up the back of my neck. I just know what she's about to say is going to be absolutely horrible.

"But when I let out the blood-curdling scream and he looked down to find... um, the barrier had been broken... he threw up. From his position on top of me. He vomited all the alcohol he'd been drinking that night, right down in my face, my mouth wide open since I had yelled out because it hurt so bad. So there I was, in excruciating pain, him still inside me, and he goes all Exorcist... in... my motherfucking... *mouth*."

NINE

DEAN

MY GUT ROILS, NOT AT THE thought of the vomit or the fact the shithead did it right in her face, although that would be fucking disgusting, but because my beautiful girl went through that. The smart, focused young woman had finally come out of her shell for one night of unadulterated fun, leaving her introvert personality behind to let loose and be a normal college kid for one party, and what happened? Probably the most traumatizing thing that had ever happened to her in her whole entire otherwise quiet, low-key life.

"What a goddamn pussy," I growl, my voice echoing in the silence of the hollow tunnel.

"What?" she squeaks, and I realize she thinks I'm talking about her, probably assuming I was calling her a pussy over the pain of losing her virginity.

"He was a fucking pussy," I clarify. "Who would vomit over the sight of a little blood, especially when they were goddamn lucky enough to be inside you?" I lean the short distance between our bodies and wrap my hand around the back of her neck, pulling her close to my face. I whisper against her lips, "If that had been me you were gifting with your first time—and no matter what you say about it not being special, it fucking is—it would have gone a lot differently. Your pussy would be the greatest gift to ever be given, whether it was your first time or not. Yeah, you could blame yourself all you want about withholding the information you'd never been with anyone before from him, but that's complete bullshit, love."

I give her a quick soft kiss on her lips before trailing across her cheek to her ear, and I feel her hands reach out and brace herself against my chest. I enjoy her shiver, growing rock-solid inside my jeans, as my hot breath tickles her ear. "Because if it had been me, you wouldn't have had to say anything." I move my lips downward, pressing them to the soft skin just below her ear, and I breathe in her intoxicating scent.

Gardenias. I would recognize it anywhere. Mr. Watson used to pick one from the garden at the orphanage and bring it to Miss Potts every day during their blooming season. The scent always reminded me of love and warmth, the same feelings I was coming to associate with the sexy woman in my arms.

I kiss a path down the column of her throat, letting my breath tease her, as I tell her, "I would've been able to tell by the way you trembled in my arms, my every touch a new feeling you'd never experienced before." I travel back up to her pouty lips, taking them heatedly, to distract her as I uncross her legs and place them on the outsides of mine, dipping my tongue in to tangle with hers as she gasps when I move forward and lay her back. I reach across her and drag the jacket over, balling it up and placing it under her head as a pillow.

I growl against her mouth, "I would've known by the blush on your perfect face as I'd feel your smooth-as-silk skin beneath my hands, when I couldn't keep them to myself any longer." I brace myself on an elbow beside her head as I reach for the hem of her tank top, placing my hand flat on her soft stomach. "And how you'd begin to pant, your heart thundering audibly when you felt me moving it upward to your amazing breasts." I enact my words, slowly gliding my hand up until I'm cupping her flesh, feeling her pebbled nipple in the center of my palm. I tweak it between the pads of my fingers, feeling her hips thrust upward as she whimpers.

I move my hand away, and the sound of her disappointed moan gives me the permission I need to lift her shirt. She shivers as her creamy skin is exposed before I take one nipple into my mouth, my erection becoming painfully hard in my jeans. Oh, how I'd love to rip them off and bury myself balls deep into her undoubtedly fist-tight pussy, but no. I'm enjoying driving her crazy, to a point I'm sure she's never felt before. So I continue with my sweet torture.

As her hands move suddenly to grip the back of my head, holding me to her, I can't help but grin around her hardened nub, grazing my teeth lightly over the sensitive peak, feeling her shudder beneath me. I suck it into my mouth before letting go with an audible pop. "I would've been able to tell by your responsiveness, your reaction to every tiny move I make," I say, feeling her jerk and grind as my calloused hand slides down her side, light enough to tickle her, making her gasp.

I lean up onto my elbow, hovering over her angelic face, her mouth open slightly as she breathes shallowly, her eyelashes fluttering with her lids closed tight. "Look at me, love," I demand, needing to see her responses clearly through her gaze, to make sure I'm only doing exactly what she wants. She opens her green eyes, glossed over with utter bliss, and I smile gently down at her before leaning down to kiss her for a brief moment.

As my hand reaches the waistband of her jeans, I pull back to watch her, while I explain, "I would've known by the way you'd suddenly hold your breath, waiting to see what I'd do next as I got rid of the only things standing in my way of your hidden treasure. Breathe, baby."

She sucks in a breath as I unbutton her jeans and lean back on my knees to untie and rid her of her pink Chucks before sliding her pants down her long, lightly muscled legs. The damn jeans are tight as fuck, but grasping the fitted ankles of the denim, I pull them off swiftly, smiling to myself when her hands fly to her light gray cotton boy shorts to keep them from being pulled off with them. The sight of them couldn't be sexier if they were a naughty black, lacy thong. They're so perfectly Emmy, and the complete opposite of what I'm used to seeing on the other women I've ever been with, since they wanted to impress me with their fancy lingerie. I almost groan in pained pleasure at how unintentionally sexy she is through her innocence, but I'm able to keep it in check, my sole focus on taking her to the brink of her comfort zone, to push her as far as I can without scaring her away.

Resuming my position on top of her, I press my hips forward, the heat of her cradling my cock, and I have no doubt she's dampening the front of my jeans. The knowledge makes me momentarily lose my grip on the reins of my control, and I take her lips in a punishing kiss for having this power over me. I feel her hands gripping my hair and her own control slipping as I grind myself against her, but not wanting to push her too far too fast, I back off once again.

I continue where I left off, moving to whisper in her ear, since she seems to love the feeling of my breath there. "I would've known, when I drove you to the point of begging for me to touch you, but were too shy to allow yourself to ask. But knowing undoubtedly that you couldn't take it anymore, I'd put you out of your misery. And the second I felt how soaked and tight you were, it would've confirmed what I already knew."

I slip my hand inside the elastic of her boy shorts, finding nothing but soft, smooth skin before I reach wetness the likes I've never felt before. She's drenched, and knowing I've done this to her, to a woman who said she's never felt desire before, that possessiveness inside me explodes, and I have to fight the urge to growl, *Mine*, as I gently sink one finger into her tight pussy.

I watch her face contort, her eyes widening before clamping shut as her back arches, her chin lifting toward the ceiling of the catacombs. Her mouth opens with her gasp, and I give her a searing kiss as I stroke inside her silken walls. When her hips start to circle against my knuckles, I add a second finger, stretching her and making her whimper.

I bite my lip to keep control over my speed and depth, determined to get her completely ready. God, her face is the most beautiful sight I've ever seen as I watch her pleasure play across her features. If I don't do something to distract myself, I'm going to come right in my jeans like a damn schoolboy. So I begin to move down her body, all while making a 'come here' motion with my fingers against that magical spot inside her, trailing kisses over her soft skin.

I use my other hand to swiftly pull her underwear off, and when I'm positioned between her legs, I can tell she's nervous, but I can also feel her determination to battle her fears. And that's when I know Emmy is mine. Six years she's lived without intimacy after her horrible first experience, and she's chosen me to help her finally overcome her past. Unfamiliar emotions consume me, making me feel animalistic. I fight the urge to mark her in some way, to let all others know she belongs to me, and only me.

This ingenious, gorgeous, remarkable woman is mine, whether she knows it yet or not.

I need to taste her. I've memorized the sight of her unrivaled face and body, her intoxicating scent. I'm addicted to the sound of her lyrical voice, with its light southern accent. I want to touch her everywhere at once, her buttery soft skin, her blazing core. The only one of my senses left to satisfy is taste, so I whisper against the lips of her pussy, "There would've been no rushing, love. There wouldn't have been any doubt. You wouldn't have been able to hide it from me. I would've tasted your innocence."

With that, I remove my fingers, replace them with my tongue, and take a long, slow swipe from the bottom of her opening, all the way up to circle her clit. And as the breath she was holding whooshes out of her and I feel her thighs quiver against my shoulders, I release the growl I've been holding back as her flavor hitting my taste buds snaps what little hold I had left on my control.

I'd wanted to take it slow, build her up to the point her sanity would've broken, but instead, without even trying, my sweet Amelia turned the tables on me. I straight up devour her, alternating between lapping at her juices, nibbling at her clit, and pushing my tongue in as far as I can to taste her, something no other man on the face of the planet ever has. She's mine, and if I can't mark her in some visible way for the world to see, then I will brand her from the inside, making it so she never wants another man for the rest of her life.

"Oh, God," she moans, as I continue to eat at her, my arms wrapping around her hips to hold her steady as her instincts take over and she grinds against my face. I fucking love it, feeling her letting go, allowing herself to enjoy what I'm doing to her, winning the war against her fears. I gently use my thumbs to pull back and completely expose her clit as I focus all my attention there, finding a light fluttering pattern with my tongue that has her back arching and her hands fisting in my hair. Every muscle in her body coils, and her breath comes out in pants, as she sobs, "Oh… oh, my God." And to finally take her over the edge, I lave at her hardened bundle of nerves, groaning against her drenched flesh as I consume her, and I feel her shatter.

I slow my tongue's assault on her pussy, but I don't stop. I can't. Not with the little gasps she makes, the sexy rolling of her hips, and the jerking of her muscles with every lick I take. So responsive. So fucking delicious. I never want this to end.

Emmy

Dear Ra, Isis, and all the gods, never have I felt such pleasure than what Dean just gifted me with, and continues to give me as he makes lazy figure eights around my clit and core with his tongue. The feeling is soothing at the bottom until he makes his teasing pass over the top, sending a shudder through me every time as he toys with the sensitive nub.

I've had self-induced orgasms before, admittedly to images of the man currently between my legs who gave me my first with another person, after waking up from dreams he would be the star of. But those didn't hold a candle to the one I just experienced. Fuck, those didn't even compare to the jolting aftershocks I keep having as he makes another pass with his mouth. And surprisingly, as he keeps circling, I grow less sensitive to the sensation, and my hips start rolling once again. But this time, I feel an overwhelming need to have something inside me.

I bite my lip as my head begins to thrash, pressing into my

jacket until my back is arching, trying to push myself closer to him. What can I do to make him understand I need to be filled, when I don't even understand the feeling myself? And as he continues his sweet torture, my hand grows a mind of its own and reaches to help me find relief. But before my fingers even reach my throbbing flesh, he grabs my hand in one of his in a vice-like grip, strong but without hurting me, and I whimper and meet his eyes.

"This pussy is mine. From now on, I'm the only one who gets to touch it. If it needs something, it'll get it from me and me alone. Does it need something, Em?" he growls against my lower lips, and it sends another jolt through me, making me shiver. I know I should be pissed, shocked, revolted at his words, but instead, I feel like the most desired woman on the face of the planet. I can't form words, and all that comes out is a low moan.

"Tell me what you want, love," he urges, and picks up his figure eights once again.

Several passes later, when I'm in a near frenzy, I finally manage to sob out a, "Please!" my cry echoing throughout the tunnel.

His mouth leaves me, and suddenly he's looming over me, and I peek up at him to find his lips glistening, his close-cropped beard framing them as his tongue darts out to lick the moisture my pussy left there. My eyes move upward to find his almost wild, and I tremble with need to find his desire and possessiveness on full display. All shyness leaves me with that look, and I find my hands reaching for his black tank. He lets me pull it off, up and over his head, and then I go for the button of his jeans.

I can feel his eyes burning into me as he allows me to do as I please, his massive, muscular arms flexing as he braces himself on his hands and knees above me, but my gaze is following what my hands are doing. I unbutton then slide down the zipper, finding black boxer briefs behind them, and hooking my thumbs into the waistband, I pull them both down over his hips until his cock springs free.

My heart skips a beat at the sheer size of him. He's much larger than Paul, but I'm so desperate to feel him inside me, I don't think twice about taking him into my hand and stroking him from root to tip. He's like velvet over steel, the skin the softest I've ever felt, enveloping an erection so hard it looks painful. My hand looks so small wrapped around his cock, and when I start to feel intimidated, I peel my eyes away to meet his.

I find him watching me closely, seeming to enjoy my exploration of the first male anatomy I've ever bothered to explore, but I can see he's fighting with himself, trying to keep still and let me make my own discoveries. That knowledge melts me, and all the feelings growing over the past few hours for this incredible man merge, and it hits me that who I thought was my enemy could actual be my one great love. He could be the Geb to my Nut, the Egyptian god of earth and goddess of sky and stars. There's a fine line between love and hate, and I realize what I'm feeling for him has plowed through that thin barrier as he's proven every single one of my old thoughts about him wrong. It was my own damn pride standing in my way, and I'd made Dean into the bad guy, when really, he was my knight in shining armor all along. It's with that thought in mind that I take a deep breath, look into his amazing eyes, and do the bravest thing I've ever done before.

"Will you make love to me?" I ask, forcing my gaze to stay locked on his, even as I feel my entire body flush.

He stares at me for a few moments, his eyes caressing every part of my face, before he lowers himself on his elbows, to whisper in my ear, "I wasn't expecting to find an angel in the catacombs, love. I don't have any protection."

I hadn't even thought about that. Six years after having sex just the one time, it wasn't something my busy brain really used up space for, but the feelings I have for this man, whose body presses closely to mine, his mutual emotions showing clearly, I feel nothing but trust for him, when I stutter, "I… I'm on birth control, for um… to keep me regulated. I uh… I got tested after— um."

"Baby, are you trying to tell me you're protected and clean?" He puts me out of my bumbling misery.

"Yes," I sigh, with a relieved smile.

"I'm clean too. But, Em, are you sure?" he asks, and I feel his hips circle against me, making my eyelids flutter. "You want me to make love to you for the first time on the dirty ground?" His eyebrows draw together, as if he's starting to question whether we should.

God, doesn't he see? "Dean, I was conceived in the Great Pyramid of Giza. These undiscovered places… these catacombs," I whisper, letting my gaze take in the tunnel around us as he stares down at me, "they make my soul happy. There is nowhere I would rather be than trapped down here with you. And the only thing that could top the fact I'm on an adventure in search of the lost Ring of Atlantis, is if you were to make love to me, right here, right n—"

His lips crash down on mine, my confession his undoing, and he reaches down to help me push his clothes all the way off before pressing himself intimately against me. I become aware of the smallest details, taking them all in and memorizing them. The feel of his hairy legs against my smooth ones. The rock-hard muscles of his body cushioned by my softness. His rough and calloused hand reaching to hold my much tinier one, bringing it up to rest above my head. His pulsing erection nuzzling the entrance of my wet heat. And my favorite, the part I will fantasize about for the rest of my life: the feel of his short beard on my neck and his hot breath tickling my ear, as he whispers, "You're mine," before slowly, carefully, inch by achingly perfect inch, he slides inside me, filling me up until I feel like I might tear in two. But there's not an ounce of pain. Just the feeling of being full to the brim, sharing my small body with a man as large as Dean.

I look up into his handsome face, forcing myself to keep my eyes on him when they want to shut in utter bliss. I want to erase my first experience and replace it with this one, with this wonderful man, in this dream of a place, the feelings rushing inside me so new and unfamiliar, but welcome. But I lose the battle with my lids when he starts to move, because it's like the feel of him stroking inside me combined with the perfection of his face is just too overwhelming all at once.

He pulls almost all the way out before thrusting back in, hitting that spot inside me that makes my head spin. I'm thankful for the way he surrounds me with his entire body, caging me in and grounding me, because so much pleasure at once is making me dizzy, not knowing which feeling to focus on, instead just trying to consume it as a whole. I pull my hand out of his so I can hold onto his bulging biceps on either side of my head, and as he leans down to trail kisses down my neck, I turn my head and open my eyes to find our matching tattoo along his forearm, and at that same moment, I feel him trace mine on my collarbone with his tongue.

My hands tighten their grip on his arms and my hips lift to meet his every thrust as he picks up speed, my gasps and moans of pleasure urging him on. I never imagined sex could feel like this. And it dawns on me that it's because I never thought about what it would be like to actually make love with a person I desired. Always too busy, always too absorbed in my schooling and chasing my dream to worry about any of this. God, who knew?

He moves one of his arms then, and I think he's about to cup my breast, but instead, he places it right in the center of my chest, closing his eyes as his movements slow back down, thrusting shallowly as he visibly concentrates. He pulls his knees up underneath himself more, to balance without bracing on his elbows, and taking my hand, he places it in the center of his chest with his other.

I feel his heart pounding there, and I smile at the fact I can bring this gorgeous man, a man who could have anyone in the world, to his knees, and I watch him, mesmerized, and he feels my heartbeat too.

"Wow, it really is true," he whispers, more to himself than to me.

He looks down at me and sees my questioning look, and when he finally speaks, my heart soars.

"One more interesting finding about The Golden Ratio in the human body, baby. The harmonics of the heart. According to Dan Winter's studies, when a person is relaxed, receptive, and feeling loved, the average distance between frequency peaks, or heartbeats, recorded was 1.618. The Golden Ratio. And when *two* people were hooked to the machine and they sent love to each other, their waves and peaks lined up at 1.618—so they were, in essence, two hearts beating as one. Therefore, when two people are sharing the emotion of real, reciprocal love, the average space between their hearts' electrical waves is 1.618, The Golden Ratio, which is, literally, eternal love."

My eyes tear up, and the all-consuming feeling of finding the one my heart belongs to overwhelms me. I take my hand from his chest, lean up to wrap it around his neck, and pull his face down to mine. I kiss him with everything I have, fleetingly wondering if there could've ever been a more perfect man for me, one who would pause during lovemaking to basically confess his feelings for me in a—admittedly nerdy but sweet—way only people like us would understand.

He sucks my bottom lip into his mouth and wraps his arm

around my lower back, yanking me downward as he thrusts up into me, and soon, a feeling starts to build within me, one I've never felt before, since the only orgasms I've ever had were through the bundle of nerves his pelvis rubs against with his every move.

"Oh, God," I breathe, feeling my arm grow weak where I have it draped around his neck, holding me upright. He must feel me starting to tremble with exertion, because he lays us back down, never stopping his mind-blowing momentum. "Oh, God…" I start chanting, quietly at first, until I cry out for the last time as I explode, while he thrusts one… two… three more times, and on the last one, he plants himself deep and grinds his hips as we fall over the edge. My world shatters apart blissfully, as I feel him pulsing, filling, and coating the inside of me, soothing me with its warmth.

He buries his face in my neck, his heart thundering against mine as we both catch our breath. "Wow," he says there, making me smile.

"Yeah. Wow," I agree, and it's like neither of us can come up with anything else to say, our minds both completely blown.

TEN

Emmy

"Finally!" The word comes out on a sigh of relief, as we'd been walking the tunnel at a snail's pace for thirty minutes, carefully checking every millimeter of the walls and floor for any sign of another clue, and had come up empty until now. "Dean, there's something over here. I can't reach it." I point at a spot about three feet above my head, shining my cell's light up the wall. I cringe, seeing the battery flash from green to red, letting me know I only have twenty percent left.

It's now 3:56 a.m. We've been down here exploring—the tunnel, and each other—for four hours. How it's possible to go from hating someone with every fiber of my being to feeling an emotion I'm afraid to admit sounds remarkably close to what people describe as love, I have no idea. But I'm not going to discount it in any way. After my parents' story, not only do I believe in instalove, but I believe in a good, old-fashioned enemies-tolovers romance with a happily ever after.

Thomas Crain and Elizabeth Davis were rival Egyptologists. They hated each other, always trying to one-up the other with their findings and records. When one of Dad's articles was published in *Smithsonian Magazine*, Mom didn't stop until hers was featured in *National Geographic*. When Mom set a record for how many hours straight spent hand-dusting a statue of Horus out of a site, Dad nearly sent himself into the hospital with caffeine-induced heart palpitations, blowing her record out of the water by a full twenty-four hours, only his was a statue of Imhotep.

This continued for years until they were both hired onto the same excavation crew, leading to that fateful day in the Great Pyramid, when they had to combine Dad's keen eye, sense of direction, and leadership skills with Mom's near genius-level ability with robotics, and precision. And together, alone one night in that dark, cold desert, almost-freezing temperature without the blazing sun shining down on them, all the stars aligned and they finally got into the queen's chamber with the crawler robot. With their adrenaline rushing, their excitement building to an all-time high, they launched themselves at each other, as Mom tells me, always with a dreamy look on her face. And as long as I remind myself to not think of them as my parents when she's reminiscing 'the best night of her life,' I can truly appreciate the magic of their story, the night I was made, a product of a match made in heaven.

Mom and Dad got married just a few weeks later, and eight months after that, I was born. They've now been together for almost a quarter of a century, so you're damn right I believe in instalove.

The tiny hairs on the back of my neck stand up, almost like metal shavings reaching for a magnet, as Dean comes up behind me. The short distance between our bodies crackles with tension, and I try my best to concentrate on keeping the light steady on the rectangular stone tile roughly the size of a shoebox just out of arm's reach.

"Up you go, love," he says in my ear, and I squeal as he ducks, wraps his arms around my thighs, and lifts me into the air.

After not even holding hands with a guy for six years, I'm still not used to Dean's freely given touch, much less him picking me up every chance he gets. I'm a little self-conscious, as my ass rests on his chest, but then I giggle and squirm as he nibbles and kisses my lower back, where my shirt has ridden up. "Oh, my God. Stop! You're going to make me pee! It's been hours!" I warn.

"Hmmm… a Golden Shower while we're in search of a ring created by the Golden Ratio. How fitting," he growls against my skin. I can't tell if he's kidding or not, until he finally stops his torture, and asks, "So what is it?"

I pull myself back to the task at hand and run my finger along the edge of the tile, feeling that it's not exactly flush with the rest of the wall. "There are no words on it like the placards before. It doesn't make any sense for this to be here," I tell him, squinting to see if I'm missing something.

"From here, before I lifted you up, it looked like there was a lip. See if it wiggles at all," he instructs, and I place my fingers on the top of the tile, and my thumb at the bottom, and alternate pressing each side, trying to tell if it'll budge. I'm being careful, not wanting to damage anything—I think I've done enough of that for one night—but then Dean suddenly licks right above the waistband of my jeans, directly in the center, where I'm guessing he's got a bird's eye view of butt cleavage, and it sends me reeling forward. My hand presses hard against the tile, forcing the bottom to pop out. But it doesn't fall to the ground. Instead, it lays flat, showing it had been covering a cubbyhole of sorts.

"Dean!" I gasp excitedly.

"I'm sorry. I couldn't help it. It's just… your ass is right here…

in my face… and your coin slot—"

"No, you crazy man. There's something in here!" I cut him off, gently sliding the tile out of the hole. "Can you take this?" I place it in his hand, his arms still wrapped around my thighs. "Move just a little bit closer. I can't make out what it is." He takes a step forward, and when I shine my cell directly into the cubby, there, in the center of its bottom, is a skeleton key about six inches long. "Oh, my God," I breathe, slowly reaching in and picking it up between my thumb and pointer finger before turning it this way and that in the light. "Dean, you've gotta see this."

He slides me down the front of his body, and I don't know what's more thrilling, the feel of his erection against the softness of my ass as my feet make their way to the ground, or the antique key I just discovered weighing heavy in my palm.

He groans, and when I turn to face him, I see him reach down and adjust himself. "You do that a lot," I observe, raising an eyebrow at him.

"Only around you, baby," he clarifies, a sexy smirk lifting one side of his lips, making my insides turn to goo. "Let's take a look."

I stare at the front of his pants, waiting for him to drop trou, but when he starts to chuckle and I lift my eyes to his, it dawns on me he's talking about the key, not his cock. "Oh." I giggle, handing it to him.

"Hmmm… cast iron. Definitely fits our timeline. So it would seem no one put this down here recently." He lifts the tile up to the light. "With the earth settling, and a century passing by, it must've made the cover fade, mismatching it and making it come unflush with the stone around it," he notes, turning it over in his hand.

"But the key. It's still in pristine condition. Like it was just made yesterday. Look. Not a scratch on the part that would fit into its lock," I point out.

"We're deep enough underground that it wouldn't be affected

by humidity and weather changes. Plus, it was inside the wall, keeping it nice and cool, and at a constant temperature. It wouldn't have rusted, expanded, or shrunk, even after all this time," he explains, and I nod in understanding.

I'm finding that learning things from a book, like in college, is a whole lot different than seeing things for yourself. Even having my degrees in archaeology and history, learning about different ores and fabrics, and their different heydays throughout the centuries, applying the things I studied for multiple-choice tests to really use 'in the field' is tricky. Seeing the key first, how perfect and clean it is, my immediate thought had been that someone recently hid it down here. It makes me realize how much I could learn from this brilliant man before me, who has nearly a decade of hands-on experience with all this stuff.

"Well, again, we have the answer, but not the question. A key, but where's the lock?" he inquires, but he says it with a mischievous glint in his eye, telling me he's excited to continue on our adventure.

As if in answer, his stomach makes a terrible noise, and I look up at him with my eyebrow lifted. "Ummm… please tell me that was a hunger growl, and not one of digestion. Because I don't know if you've noticed or not, but there aren't any facilities to use down here," I tell him.

"Definitely hunger, love. I haven't eaten anything since lunchtime," he replies with a chuckle.

"Okay, good. Because I've had to pee for the last two hours, and my bladder is about to pop. I can only imagine if one of us had to go… boom-boom," I say, shaking my head.

"Boom-boom?" he repeats, throwing his head back and letting out a laugh that makes me grin.

I open my sparkly backpack and hand it to him. "Shut up. Did you forget I brought snacks? Thank the tequila. Actually, don't thank tequila, since it's because of it I have to pee. Help yourself," I offer.

As he grabs a bag of chips out, he points down the tunnel the way we came. "If you really have to go, just pop a squat."

I look at him, horrified. "Pee… in here? Like… just on the ground?"

"Well, yeah, babe. You made an entire room collapse. What's a little urine?" His voice holds amusement that warms me as much as his words embarrass me. "I'll give you privacy, if that's what you're worried about. Just go back a ways, and I'll stay here and raid your pantry purse." He chuckles.

He's so nonchalant about it that the idea starts to grow on me. My bladder has been growing sore from being full ever since we… made love? Yes, made love. That's exactly what we did. It wasn't just sex we had. Definitely not 'fucking.' What we shared was special, soul-deep, a connection between much more than just our physical bodies. I feel a level of trust with him that I've never had with anyone before, even more than what I have with Erin, my soul sister. So if he's telling me relieving myself is okay, then I'm going to listen.

As I turn to head back up the tunnel, he grabs my hand and pulls me back to him. I look up into those beautiful eyes of his in question. "Don't make this weird, love. Okay?" he prompts.

I swallow, already feeling my hackles rise. "Okay."

"In that giant, loud purse of yours, do you have any napkins, a pack of tissues maybe?" He drops the backpack and pushes my hair behind my ear then rests his hand on the back of my neck.

"Um… y-yeah. I think so. I-uh… do you need some for your hands? I-um… I usually just suck the Dorito cheese off my fingers," I ramble.

"No, Em. When you go, you're going to need them. To clean up." He leans down and presses his lips to mine before pulling back slightly to whisper, "I came inside you, love. It would probably feel uncomfortable if you didn't have something to clean up with. If you didn't have anything in your purse, I was going to offer you my shirt."

"You… you would give me your shirt to clean up with, just so I wouldn't have to be uncomfortable after I…?" My words trail off as I look up into Dean's sincere face. The man I thought I hated mere hours ago, is now offering me the shirt off his back to take care of the mess we made together when we made love. Something I hadn't thought about in the least. Something he could've just blown off, seeing how he wouldn't be the uncomfortable one. I mean, I've never felt what it's like to have a man's cum come out of me, having never had any *in* me before, but I can't imagine it being too pleasant having to walk around with soaking wet panties.

"I'd do anything for you, love," he mumbles against my lips before kissing me deeply, sending tingles down my spine as he caresses my neck with his strong, calloused hand. He pulls back then, smiles down at me, where I'm completely speechless, and then turns me, sending me on my way up the tunnel with a swat to my ass.

I shuffle away from him in a stupor. The man is a complete conundrum. The absolute opposite of what I always envisioned him as. He's not the selfish, good-for-nothing asshole with a stupid face that I'd called him in the bar when I was venting to Erin. He's pretty much as far from that as he could possibly be. Selfish? Hell no. He literally offered me the shirt off his back. Good-for-nothing? Fuck that! He saved my life. Not to mention he gave me the best orgasms I've ever had in my life. Yep, he's definitely good for something. Stupid face? Dear Lord, no. *Nononononono.* His face would make angels weep at its beauty. And there's nothing stupid about the man. How wrong I have been about him. And how easily he forgave me for it. *'I'd do anything for you, love.'*

Thinking about it, there's probably very little I wouldn't do for Dean Savageman either. At least, not that I can think of right now.

I glance behind me, seeing he's plopped down on the ground facing the opposite direction. He brings the small bag of chips up to his mouth and leans his head back, and I smile. I'm glad I had something to offer him after everything he's done for me while we've been trapped down here.

Walking a couple more yards away, I stop and pull out the pack of wet wipes I always carry in my purse, and then set my bag on the ground. I move down the tunnel just a little ways more, not wanting to get anything on my Kate Spade, turn to make sure Dean is still in his same spot, and then wiggle my jeans down.

Hm... I've never not peed in a toilet before. How the hell am I supposed to take care of business without taking my jeans all the way off? But that's way too much damn work, stupid skinny jeans. What to do, what to do...? Then it hits me. I back up against the wall and slide down it, acting like I'm sitting in a chair. I shuffle my feet out in front of me more so I don't get my pants wet, and as I feel the burn in my legs from holding the position, I pray they don't give out while I relieve myself.

For once, disaster doesn't strike, and I clean myself up, pull up my jeans, and carry the wet wipes to my purse. I stuff them back into the packaging, and seal it closed. I'll have to remember to throw the pack away once we get out of here. With a smile on my face and a skip in my step, I hurry back to Dean, feeling much better with an empty bladder. When he stands, he leans down to peck me on the lips before heading in the direction from which I just came. "My turn," he calls over his shoulder.

My smile dies. "Wait!" I yell.

He turns, a look of concern on his face. "What? What's wrong?" He rushes back to me.

"I-uh…" Oh, God. I'm such a goob. Could I be any more awkward?

"What, love?" he prompts.

"I… I don't want you to see," I say quietly.

His brow furrows. "See what?"

My hands flop against my thighs. "Ugh! I don't want you to see my puddle!" I confess, exasperated at myself.

His lips pull in, making a straight line out of his mouth, and I can see a vein in his neck pop out. He's trying so hard not to laugh at me. But then he fails. Miserably. He laughs from deep in his belly, going so far as to reach out and hold on to my shoulder as he bends over and tries to catch his breath. "Oh, my God. You're so fucking adorable." He wipes the corner of his eye, as if he'd laughed so hard tears had formed, and I can't help the smile that spreads across my face. "I'm sure it's soaked in by now. And now I *really* gotta go." He gives me a quick kiss then turns and hurries away.

DEAN

I CAN'T WIPE THE STUPID grin off my face. The woman is a conundrum. For someone who was so quick to bite my head off and rip me a new one, she's got an undeniable sweetness to her. Where most women I've come in contact with for the past several years try to impress me with their sex appeal and overbearing confidence, Emmy's brand of sweet is a breath of fresh air. So intelligent, so clever, yet oh so innocent when it comes to dealing with a man.

Yet I love it when her temper flares and her feistiness comes out to play, so when I get a distance away, even though I really don't see it, I call back to her, "Oh, my *God!* That's the biggest puddle of piss I've ever seen! How much tequila did you drink?"

And just like I was hoping, her mortified groan and response of, "Oh, my God! Stop! It is not!" comes hurtling up the tunnel to me. I burst out laughing, and hear her snap, "I hate you a little bit right now." I finish my business, zip up my jeans, and make my way back to her, a wicked smile on my face. When I'm within arm's reach, I receive a swat to my chest, followed by the sight of Emmy shaking out her hand with a pained look on her face. "Ouch. Dick."

I lean down and steal a kiss before she tries to hit me again, apparently not learning her lesson the first time. I learned early on in my career that in order to do all the adventurous things in my show, everything from rock climbing to hiking for miles upon miles, that I needed to stay in really good shape. Glancing down at my watch, 4:32 a.m., I see it's the normal time I'm usually up and starting my morning run. Then after cardio, I'd spend the next hour weight training, a different muscle group each day. Today would have been leg day. I *never* skip leg day. I always find it hilarious when guys come into the gym, and they work out their upper body so hard, with huge, bulging biceps, pecs that could crush walnuts, and traps and lats so big it makes you wonder if they can even reach their back if they have an itch… and then you look down and they have these skinny little bird legs. Watson and I call them Johnnys, as in Johnny Bravo.

When Mrs. Potts passed away a few years ago, I adopted Watson much like he did me all those years ago. Without the love of his life to spend his days with there in that giant home, I took him on the road with me. The man was already in great shape from having a very active lifestyle, first as a miner, and then as the groundskeeper of the boys' home, so it was no surprise when we discovered he could kick ass at the gym. His body is just as fit as mine.

His official title is Personal Assistant, one I gave him so he'd accept the salary I deposit into his bank account, but really, I just love having him with me everywhere I go. Especially since he's getting up there in years. The old man's seventieth birthday is next month, and it calms my soul to know I am spending every moment I can with him, taking him on escapades and letting him see everything he could possibly want to. We checked off everything on his bucket list the first year he spent traveling with me, and I forced him to make a new one, after I taught him how to Google search on his new iPad. He's more than just a father figure. He's my guardian angel, right here on Earth. And I can't wait for him to meet Emmy.

Thinking of Watson meeting Emmy, I'm sure he'll be up in a couple hours at our hotel. He'll start looking for me, and then call Mr. Hosea, who will probably already realize I never came out of the catacombs, and they'll eventually get us out of here. In a way, that makes me kind of sad. I like being trapped down here, alone with Emmy. It's like we're in our own little world, on this adventure together, where nothing and no one else exists.

"So, a lock," Emmy says, bringing me out of my thoughts. "Can you tell by looking at it if the key is one that fits into a door, or maybe a padlock? It would be nice to have some sort of clue as to what we should be looking for."

I take the key out of her hand to take a closer look, but come up blank. "No, not really. I would assume, just because of its larger size, that it would be to a door, since nowadays padlock keys tend to be smaller than those that unlock doors. But I've come across keys this large that went to giant antique padlocks, like when I went to Arkansas and explored—"

"Fort Smith Prison. Yeah," she finishes my sentence, nodding her head as she looks at the cast iron key in my hand, and a smile spreads across my face. When I don't say anything else, she glances up at me, seeing my grin and my eyes staring down at her. Her head jerks back a little, her face twisting up. "What? Do I have something—?" Her hand flies to her nose, pinching it shut, and I laugh.

"No, love. You don't have a bat in the cave. You watch my show." I smirk.

She furrows her brows. "I told you I watch your sh—"

"Negative, Ghost Rider. You named me off the places you and I had run into each other. You never said anything about being one of my viewers," I chide, and I can feel the mischief taking over my features.

Her face turns a delightful shade of rose, and her mouth opens and closes like a fish out of water. Finally, the dam breaks. "Ugh, you brat! Yes! I watch your damn show. I've seen every episode at least ten times. And with every viewing, I watched with equal parts of awe and hatred. Erin and I even made a drinking game out of it."

My face immediately falls, and before I can catch my tone, I growl, "Who the hell is Aaron?" that unfamiliar feeling of jealousy filling my chest with fire once again.

She arches her brow at me, blinks, and then understanding comes over her face. It's her turn to smirk. "*Erin.* My roommate and best friend." When she sees that explanation isn't good enough, she adds, "My soul *sister.*"

My tense body instantly relaxes, leaving me feeling a little embarrassed, so I clear my throat and pretend it never happened. "So what's the drinking game?"

"Huh? Oh! Well, let's see." She starts ticking off on her fingers the things that would require you to take a shot. "Any time the title *No Trespassing* is said. Which is before *and* after each commercial break. We always make fun of the way you look into the camera like Zoolander and say, 'We'll be back with more *No Trespassing*, after this word from our sponsors,' and then 'Welcome back to *No Trespassing*.'" She cackles, shaking her head. "What really sucks is watching it on Netflix, when there are no commercials, so you have to take shots back-to-back."

I want to be offended, but her beautiful face doing an impression of Blue Steel while she was mimicking me makes me laugh. "What else?"

"Every time they bleep out a curse word. That's probably the most brutal rule. Especially when you combine it with 'Take a shot when Dean nearly falls or otherwise hurts himself.' You really should be more careful," she playfully scolds, then adds, "Potty mouth."

I grin and take a step closer, bringing her body flush against my front. "You love my filthy mouth," I murmur, wrapping my arms around the small of her back. I want to puff out my chest a bit when I hear and see her actually gulp, her breath catching. I love how she unconsciously responds to me. But suddenly, her face turns beet red and her eyes widen, and I feel her legs jerk against the front of mine. She tries to pull away, but I tighten my grip. "What, love? What's wrong?"

She presses her hands against my chest and tries to shove me off, but still, I don't let go. "Dean, get off," she gripes, struggling against me.

"Not until you tell me what's the matter," I grit out.

Her body goes limp against me as she gives up her fight. She buries her face in my chest and lets out a big, dramatic sigh. "I g- a we-y," she mumbles into my shirt.

"What? I couldn't make out what you said," I tell her, trying to pull her head back a little, but she holds on tight.

This time, she yells it, "I got a wetty!" and I nearly choke on my spit as I suck in air.

"A… a *wetty*?" My voice comes out almost squeaky as I try to hold in my laughter.

She pulls her face back to glower at me. "Ugh! Dean! Guys get woodies, girls get wetties! God, you suck so bad!" And she plants her face back where it was, right in the center of my chest.

For her sake, I manage to swallow the howls of laughter I want to let loose, and rub my hand up and down her back soothingly. It allows me time for the actual meaning of her words to sink in past their humor, and I groan.

I made her wet.

Right now, she's wet. For me.

My dick hardens behind my zipper. Again.

"Can we continue on our exploration now, before I die of embarrassment?" she grumbles, tilting her head to the side so I can hear her.

I kiss the top of her hair, breathing in her scent, before giving her a playful smack on her ass and stepping back, where I adjust myself. Again. But before she can comment, I tell her, "Let's do it," then bend down to pick up the bags, throwing them over my shoulder.

She clears her throat. "At least we're looking for something big enough to fit this key, right? I mean, that should be easier to spot than these tiny clues we've been finding. My phone's nearly dead, so not much more flashlight time left," she rambles, clearly trying to get her mind off her 'wetty' and my 'woody'.

"You would think. Unless the door or lock or whatever is hidden behind something, like the cubbyhole we found the key in," I say. "I have an idea though." She looks up at me, her face questioning. "I'm actually kind of curious to see what's at the end of this thing. How about we head straight for the back, take a look around, and then backtrack?"

She shrugs. "Sounds good to me."

With that settled, I reach out and lace my fingers through hers, tugging her closer to my side. I catch a glimpse of the small smile she tries to hide, turning her face away from me, and we start our trek.

We walk for a while, the distance going by a lot faster since we aren't scouring the walls with a fine-tooth comb, and soon, the tunnel spills out into a room much like the one in the very front, wide and open, with a much higher ceiling.

Except this one's walls are filled.

Filled with row after row of bones.

ELEVEN

Emmy

"Oh, my God," I breathe, pulling my hand out of Dean's and making my way to the very center of the huge chamber. I spin slowly, taking in the haunting beauty of the sight before me. Bones the color of clouds passing over a full moon line the walls, floor-to-ceiling. Stacked in patterns, creating works of art out of the people's remains.

"Hmm...," I hear Dean say behind me, and I turn to see him bending over and looking closely at the wall of bones. He turns to smile at me. "All tibias and femurs. That's why it's so beautifully symmetrical."

I glance upward at the ceiling, the light fixtures still hiding flawlessly, but the way it's casting shadows above the bones, you can tell the actual walls of the chamber are much farther back than the one created by the remains. "Just like in Paris. The tibias, femurs, and skulls are used to make the barriers that hold the rest of the skeletal parts behind them," I note, something I'm sure he already knows. I turn to watch him walk across the room to where there's a large stone placard. It looks as big as a gravestone, which I guess technically it would be.

"Ah, here we go. 'St. Charles Cemetery, 1782,'" he reads. "These are the original occupants of the cemetery that filled up, and they got the idea to dig the catacombs."

"But there's gotta be way more deceased here than just one cemetery's worth," I point out, looking around for another gravestone. "Look how many skulls. There has to be thousands of skeletons in this chamber."

"There," Dean calls, and when I look back at him, he's pointing across the room. This stone is much smaller, and when I take a glance around, I see there are a few more this size around the perimeter. They're hard to see in the dim lighting, because they're the exact color of the bones framing them.

"'Yellow Fever Epidemic, 1853,'" I recite.

From his position in front of another sign, he calls, "'Yellow Fever Epidemic, 1878.'"

"'Cholera Epidemic, 1832.'" God, I wish I had my camera right now. I would love to be documenting all the formations and placards. I'd use my phone, but with its low battery, I want to save it in case we need the light.

"Hmm... I'm not really sure about this one. 'Carville, 1850-1900,'" he reads, and it's thrilling when it dawns on me I know something else he doesn't know.

"Carville is where there was a hospital designated to the study of leprosy, and also the Louisiana Leper Home," I explain, and he nods, a proud look on his face that warms me to my core.

We spend a few minutes walking around the perimeter, pointing out different designs made out of the bones, or a skull with interesting features, and when we've taken it all in, we look at each other with mirrored faces full of wonder. Our souls are happy, and it makes me smile that even after years of doing this on his show, Dean still seems so thrilled by our exploration.

"But… I don't see a door or any sort of lo—"

"Holy shit," I interrupt, my mouth falling open at something my eye just happened to catch at the exact moment Dean sounded like he was about to lose hope of finding anything in here, which would force us to backtrack. I point up at the ceiling, and Dean comes to stand beside me, looking in the direction of my finger.

"What is it? I don't see anything," he says, and I glance up at him to see him squinting.

When I look back up, what I saw is gone. *Surely…* I shake my head, trying to clear my vision. When I check again, I see just a sliver of the image. Ah, good. I knew I wasn't seeing things. I try Dean's idea and squint, but it doesn't become any clearer until I slightly adjust my feet, spreading them farther apart and making me a tiny bit lower. "There!" I grab his arm and tug, trying to pull him down to where he's at my eye level. "Now look at the ceiling, just a little ways behind the wall of bones. When the light hits it just right…"

"1618," he breathes next to my face, and I grin, excited that he can see it too. "You know what that means, right?"

My brow furrows. "They've written it to look like another year marker, but I'm more than a little certain it's another clue on our Golden Ratio scavenger hunt," I tell him, the 'duh' clear in my voice.

I feel him turn toward me, so I face him, seeing his gorgeous eyes dancing with mirth. "Yeah, love. And it means you're going bone climbing, and not the kind you'll be doing later, if I have anything to do with it."

DEAN

I watch, enjoying the flush that covers Emmy's face, and even more so the giggle that bubbles up and pours out of her at my lame come-on.

Shaking her head, she swats my chest, gentler this time, so she doesn't hurt her hand. She places her fists on her hips, checking over the wall of bones directly in front of us. After a moment, she turns to me. "How the hell am I going to get up there? The bones have to be fragile, being at least a century old. I mean, it's one thing to destroy part of the catacombs themselves. That can possibly be fixable. Right? Yeah. But the bones… Like, once they're damaged, there's no fixing that."

"Then here's what we're going to do. I'm going to lift you up there, and you just take a peek to see if there's even anything behind the wall of bones. Let's start there, and then figure out what to do next when the time comes," I tell her, soothing her nerves.

She nods vigorously. "Yes, sounds good."

I get behind her like I did before in the tunnel, duck down, and hoist her up on my shoulders, standing with ease. She must be getting used to me picking her up, because she doesn't let out her usual girlish squeal. I can't help it though. She's so small, so feminine, so easy for me to lift and put her exactly where I want her. I can feel the heat between her legs resting around my neck and shoulders, and that same possessive feeling comes over me, knowing I'd filled her up, consumed her, taken ov—

"Dean? You gotta walk forward. I can't see anything from back here," she cuts into my dirty thoughts, and I move toward the skulls, femurs, and tibias.

"What do you see?" I ask her, growing excited.

"Nothing yet. I'm still a little too low," she mumbles.

"Stand on my shoulders."

"What?" she squawks, tightening her grip around my chin.

"Stand on my shoulders, love. I won't let you fall. Trust me," I tell her, and it's the truth. I feel fiercely protective over Emmy, and it would be over my dead body that anything happens to her.

"Promise? You're really tall, and that would be a really long drop to a really hard ground," she points out, but I hear that she's conceding to the idea.

"I swear. I won't let you get hurt, Emmy."

"O-okay." She adjusts herself on my shoulders and lifts one foot then pauses. "Um… how the hell do I get up there? I was the furthest thing from a cheerleader as you could get in school."

I chuckle then lift my hands up at her sides, palms up. "Here, give me your hands." She hesitantly lets go of my chin and places her hands in mine. "Now get your left foot on my shoulder for leverage, and then push off with it and our hands to get your right one up."

"Oh shit," she whimpers, but she begins to follow my instructions.

When she's got her left foot up, I feel her tremble, so I give her some help. "On the count of three, love. Ready? One… two… three." And as she lumbers up, I push upward with my hands, lending my strength to help her lift herself.

Squatting on my shoulders, she then asks, "Now what?"

"Now, you stand. Hang onto my chin again, and I'm going to take hold of your ankles to help you balance, then stand right up. I'm not going anywhere. I'm not going to let you fall. I am the fucking Great Wall of China right now, baby. Not going to budge," I assure her, and I feel her death grip on my hands loosen.

Ever so slowly, she wraps her palms back around my head and

I grasp a hold of her slender ankles, pulling her feet downward onto my shoulders more firmly, making her feel steady. And with great care and unhurried movements, she finally stands to her full height. "I did it," she whispers excitedly.

"You did it, love. Now, what do you see?"

"It's hard to see with all the shadows. One sec. I'm getting my cell out of my pocket. I have just enough juice left for a few more minutes of light," she explains. I hear the phone's unlocking sound, and see the area around us brighten. "Dean! Oh, my God!"

I tighten my grip on her legs as she jerks with excitement. "What? What is it?"

"It's a door! There aren't any skeletons behind this section of the bone wall. It's clear for a width of about six feet. And it looks…"

Her words trail off, and the suspense is killing me. "Emmy," I gush.

"Sorry! It looks like there is metal behind this section of bones. And the bones themselves are only about half of their actual length," she describes.

"Hidden gate," I breathe.

"What?" she asks, and I can tell she's looking down at me by the volume of her voice, so I look up at her.

"Hidden gate. The bones must be attached to the metal, making it look like the rest of the wall, but it must swing open. Look for hinges on the inside," I tell her, and I feel her adjust herself.

"Yes! There are hinges here on the left side!" She leans the other way carefully. "And the metal ends at this row of skulls." She points, and I grab my wallet out of my back pocket and drop it on the ground in front of the correct column to mark it.

"Awesome, okay, let's get you down." She squats back down, grasps my lifted hands, and then climbs down my back, her eagerness obviously outweighing her nervousness. I swing her around to my front and pull her flush against me. I dip my face to her neck and nuzzle her there, before whispering, "I told you I wouldn't let you fall."

She shivers, and smiles up at me when I lift my face. "I don't know why, but I trust you, Dean. Thank you for not letting me get hurt," she says quietly, and her confession floods my chest with warmth. Her face softens, seeing her words affected me, and I lower my lips to hers, marking this moment with a sweet and lingering kiss.

Finally, I pull back and we look at the wall of bones. I step up to where my wallet is on the ground, bend to pick it up, and with it in my hand, I follow the column of skulls. I absently hear Emmy move away. I don't see anything out of place. No way of opening the hidden gate. I put my wallet in my back pocket then rub the back of my neck. What now?

"Dean," Emmy says, and she bends a little at the waist, squinting her eyes.

"You know, any other time a woman would bend and squint her eyes at my hips like that, it would give me a complex. But since you know for a fact what I have in my pa—"

"Dean!" she scoffs, but I see amusement in her eyes and at the corners of her lips. "Come here, you turd. I'm not looking at your cock."

That word coming out of her mouth makes the appendage in question twitch, but I do as I'm told, coming to stand next to her.

"Stay there," she orders, then paces forward. "This skull." She points to one on the row my wallet had marked that looks just like all the others, until I look more closely and see— "One eye socket is larger than the other, no? Or is just me?"

"No, you're right. It's definitely bigger." I move toward her. "Where's your phone?"

She hands it to me after turning the light on, and it makes a beeping sound as 10 percent flashes across the screen. I drop to my knees on the ground and come face-to-face with the skull, getting a better angle, and when I shine the beam of light into the larger eye socket, lo and behold….

"There's a goddamn keyhole!" I jump to my feet, wrap my arms around her, and swing her around. "Emmy, my love, you found the keyhole! You put together all these clues, you spotted the secret 1618 hidden in the ceiling, and you found the door. You. Found." I kiss her left cheek. "The fucking." I kiss her right cheek, loving the sound of her giggle. "Keyhole!" I devour her mouth in a searing kiss that leaves us both breathless. When I release her once more, her face is flushed and her breath comes out in quick pants. "You do the honors. You're the one who's put all this together. This is your discovery."

Never have I been so excited for another person before. Any other time, it would have been a fight to the death to get to the goal first. But not with Emmy. She deserves this. She should be the one to open the door.

"The key," she says, more to herself than to me. She pats her pockets, and then rubs her forehead, thinking.

"Right here, love." I pull the long, iron key out of my pocket and hold it out to her in the palm of my hand.

"Right. Thanks. I'm… I'm a little overwhelmed," she confides. "I mean, this is huge, you know? Like, this stuff is all hidden. This key was hidden in the wall. This is a secret gate masked by human remains that leads to another hidden door that leads to God knows what, Dean. Like… none of this is in the catacombs' history. And none of this was on the map, right?"

"Right," I confirm with a nod.

"We'll be the first people to see this since it was sealed up over a century ago. This… this is a big deal," she says quietly, looking down at the key in her hand.

I walk up to her and lift her gaze to mine with a finger beneath her chin. "It is. It's a big deal. And it was all you. When we get out of here, the world is going to know *you* were the one who found whatever we're about to discover."

She audibly gulps. "Oh shit."

"What?" I ask, confused.

"I hadn't even thought of that. Dean, we're going to be all over the news when we're rescued." She shakes her head. "I... I don't like attention. Shit, I don't even go anywhere except the little hole in the wall pub right by my house. Look at the profession I chose! I like abandoned places no one even knows exist. And then I go home and work anonymously behind my computer. My dream was to have the most badass archaeology blog on the internet. I have no desire for people to actually see *me*."

"I'll be right there with you, love. I'm not going to let anything happen to you," I assure her, not quite understanding her fear of the limelight.

"Dean, you don't get it. I'm an only child. I grew up with my parents, who were gone a lot of the time, and my Gran, who raised me while they were on a dig. I've had two whole friends my entire life. I've been to exactly one party, and you know how well that went." Panic rises steadily in her voice and hand gestures. "Yes, I live in this crazy, crowded tourist spot of a city, but I'm gone all the time, trying my best to sneak into these forgotten places, so I can be alone inside them. Their history is the only company I desire. And when I'm home, I'm usually locked inside my room, working on my blog, or scouring the internet, looking for somewhere else to go hide. I don't want to be the center of attention. I...."

Her voice trails off as she visibly trembles. I wrap my arms around her, hating the sight of her so shaken. I'd do *anything* to take away her fear. *Anything* to bring back the bright-eyed excitement from only minutes before.

"I want you to tell them you discovered it. You found all the clues and figured out what they led to," she says.

Anything... but that.

"No," I state, the tone in my voice leaving no room for argument, but she presses on just the same.

"Please, Dean. I don't want—"

"No way, Emmy. There's no way I'm taking credit for something so huge, when I'm not the one who found it. The guilt wouldn't be worth it. And you may not believe me now, but eventually, you would grow bitter. You might not think so now. You might think you want me to take the glory for this discovery, so you don't have to be in the spotlight. But you would come to despise me for it. You said you trust me. Well, trust me on this, love." I squeeze her tighter. "I swear to you, I will be by your side through everything. I will literally hold your hand through it all. But this is *yours*."

She's silent for a few moments, but then I feel her relax and melt against me. "You promise?" she whispers into my chest.

I rub my hands up and down her back. "I promise. Every second, I will be right there." When I feel her nod, I try to lighten the mood. "Plus, with me standing there, no one will be looking at you anyways. I'm the rock star of documentaries, remember?"

I hear her gasp, and then feel her start to shake, finally hearing her giggle into my shirt. She leans back, and her eyes are sparkling with mirth, and I grin.

"You're such a dickhead," she laughs. "Not a selfish, site-stealing one, but a dickhead nonetheless."

"Hey, I can't help I'm kind of a big deal," I tell her, earning another smack to the chest. There's my feisty girl.

"Ugh. Okay." She pulls out of my embrace and shakes herself, leaning her head toward one shoulder then the other. Then she brings one arm across her chest, pulling it closer to her body with the opposite hand wrapped around her bicep, and proceeds to switch to the other, stretching herself out. I watch on in amusement as she does a couple squats, sucking and blowing out air like she's doing deadlifts.

"Um… Em. Whatcha doin', love?" I ask, as she does some lunges across the center of the chamber.

"Have you never seen *Tomb Raider? National Treasure?* For fuck's sake, *Raiders of the Lost Ark?* We don't know what's behind that door! I'm stretching in case we have to run from a boulder, or dive under swinging axes, or God knows what else. Shit could be booby-trapped," she explains, jogging in place, her face completely serious.

I bite my lip in an attempt to hold it in, but I just can't. I fold in half, hands on knees, and bellow with laughter. And I don't stop until tears form at the corners of my eyes. Dear God, no woman on the face of the planet has ever made me laugh as hard or as much as the beautiful creature in front of me, currently glaring at me as she does a couple jumping jacks. And what makes her even more delightful is she doesn't mean to be funny. How she's able to be adorably cute but sexy as fuck is beyond my comprehension, but she's nailed it either way.

When I catch my breath, I gesture toward the skull hiding the keyhole. "All right, Lara Croft. Let's do this."

She does one last set of Heisman circuits, and then finally makes her way over to me. Hesitating once more, she looks up at me with those gorgeous green eyes. "What if it doesn't fit?"

"Amelia Suvan Crain," I growl, and she jerks, arching a brow at me. "If you don't stick that key into that hole right now, I will tackle you to the ground and fuck you after forcing me to watch those perfect tits bounce around during the little Insanity workout you just did. Four words, love: White. Tank. No. Bra." She glances down, clearly having forgotten what she was wearing, and her cheeks turn that beautiful shade of rose I've come to love.

I lean down next to her ear, letting my lips graze its shell as I add, "And you're all stretched out and warmed up now, so I'm sure I could put you into all sorts of creative positions you've never even heard of."

She shudders, closing her eyes and unconsciously rolling her hips against mine, and I groan when she bites her lip. The sound snaps her out of it, and she clears her throat nervously as she reaches around me with the key toward the skull.

I step away so she can carefully insert the key into the oversized eye socket without damaging the bone. The tip of her dark pink tongue pokes out of the corner of her lips, a look of concentration coming over her delicate features. She moves the hand holding the key in a tiny circle, trying to line it up correctly, and finally, the long stem of the skeleton key slides in up to the intricately designed end. We both take a deep breath, holding it in when she turns the key, then let it out with a whoosh as the lock makes a satisfying *snick-clink*.

"Now what?" she whispers, apparently still scared of the door being booby-trapped in some way.

I look at the wall of bones, and then her hand still holding the key inserted in the skull. "I'd say push. It would have to open inward, because if it opened outward, with the bones being so closely stacked together, either it wouldn't move, or it would destroy two columns of skulls as it crushed them together."

She doesn't move. She just stands staring at her hand as it trembles grasping the key. Finally, she looks up at me. "Dean, you do it." Her eyes are pleading. "I'm scared."

Those words almost send me into action, doing as she pleads, but I don't want to take this moment away from her. She'd regret it in the end. "No, love. It's all yours. How long have you wanted this? How long have you wanted to beat me to making one of these discoveries? And now you've earned it. I'm not going to take that away from you."

"But—"

"Ain't happenin', Em," I say firmly. But in a gentler tone, I add, "Our tattoos. Our Atlantean Rings. What happened to Howard when he was the only one wearing the symbol when they entered King Tut's tomb?"

"He was the only one who lived to old age," she answers quietly.

"What happened to everyone else?"

"They all died mysteriously within a couple years of the discovery. He was the only one protected," she replies, and I nod.

"And he was only *wearing* the symbol. We've got that shit permanently inked into our skin, so it's like… extra strength. Right?" I raise my eyebrows at her, prompting her to respond.

She smiles coyly, and my heart does a thing. I don't know if it drops, speeds up, stops, or what. I just know it feels… funny. When she looks at me like that, with those sparkling, trust-filled eyes, I feel myself fall for her more and more. I'm such a goner.

"Right," she agrees, and while staring up into my eyes, she pushes.

TWELVE

Emmy

I WATCH DEAN'S EYES LEAVE mine and fall to my hand as I put weight against the now unlocked, camouflaged gateway. It only wiggles at first, but the little movement causes my excitement to grow, ebbing away the nerves that had filled me moments ago.

I push harder, being careful to put the force directly into the key. I'm scared to touch the skull itself, not wanting to damage it in any way. But it still doesn't open.

"It's been sealed for a lot of years, love. You're going to have to put some strength behind it. Skulls are strong, so don't be afraid to touch them." He comes over to me, takes my hand off the key, and places my palm on the forehead of one of the skulls at my eye level, and then my other hand on one near my hips. "Now, push. Hard," he instructs, and I do as I'm told.

I put all my weight against it, and with a squeaking slide of metal against metal and ancient hinges creaking, the gate of skulls and leg bones opens inward, revealing the iron door behind it.

"Oh, my gosh," I breathe, looking up at Dean with wide eyes.

"Don't stop there, Em. Grab the key!"

The eagerness in his voice is contagious, and I hop to pull the key out of the skull's eye socket, yet remembering to be careful not to damage it with the metal. Dean follows me as I hustle up to the door, seeing the keyhole thankfully looks like it matches the gate's. To get this close and have to wait to find another key would be pure torture. I insert it into the lock, twist, grasp hold of the metal handle, and give it a yank. The same screech of metal echoes throughout the chamber as the door slides open, and I peer into the darkness beyond.

Dean's hand grasps the edge of the door above my head and opens it wider, being careful to not let it hit the still-open bone-covered gate. Obviously, there's no lighting system, since no one knew this place existed. "Shit. My phone is almost dead. How are we going to see in there?"

Dean reaches into his pocket, and I think he's going to pull out his own phone, but he reveals a lighter instead. "We're going to make a torch," he tells me, with a wink and grin.

"Out of what, exactly?" I ask. He turns to the right and looks up at the wall of femurs and tibias. "No way! Do you know how much bad juju it would bring on your head to burn someone's bones? There's got to be another source." I look around. Then up at the ceiling. "Wait a second."

"What's the matter?" Dean asks, seeing the look of confusion on my face.

"The lights are installed in the ceiling, against the back wall, not the wall of bones four feet that way," I say, pointing toward the center of the chamber. "How did no one know about this door? They would have seen it while they were installing the lights."

"Not necessarily. Look. The lights are put in about every—

what is that, twelve to fourteen feet would you say? It could've been pretty dark in here while they were working, and this clearing seems to be directly in the center of two light sources." He points at the two flat fixtures in the ceiling on either side of us. "Unless they were looking for it, it could easily have been missed. Like we said before, this isn't on any map."

I nod, agreeing with his assessment. "And you said each one has its own power source, right?"

"Yeah…?" he says, his tone questioning where I'm going with this.

"If we can get to one of the fixtures, you think we could pull it out and take it in there with us? It would save us from having to burn anything.

He looks down at me and his face goes soft. "I fucking love your brain," he tells me quietly, his eyes twinkling.

I feel my face flush and I smile shyly. "It works sometimes," I reply.

"Seems like it works a hell of a lot of the time," he corrects, and next thing I know, he's spinning me by the shoulders and I'm up on his, being hoisted into the air once again. "Up you go, love." He holds his hands up to me, and this time I know the drill. I place my palms in his, lift my feet to his shoulders, and stand, so easily this time it's like we're stunt doubles in the movie *Bring It On*. "Can you reach it?" he asks from below, after he comes flush with the corner made out of a stone wall on one side, and another made of bones perpendicular.

I reach my hand out, but it's about three feet away, and too high out of my grasp. "No. Son of a bitch," I gripe.

"How high are the rest of the skeletal remains inside the femur and tibia walls?"

"To the top," I say. My turn to wonder where his line of thinking is going.

"It's stacked completely full?" he questions.

"Yeees," I drawl. "It looks almost flat on top it's so packed."

"Crawl across the top."

"Dean, I—"

"Would you rather burn bones and risk bad juju, my voodoo queen, or crawl across carefully, only risking snapping a couple collarbones and fingers?" he cuts me off.

"Uuuugggh," I groan. "I hate you a little right now. Just so you know."

"Well then we have a love/hate relationship right now, baby. Now get your sexy ass up there," he commands, and my eyes widen. Did he just—

He doesn't give me time to think about it, as he grasps my ankles and starts to lift me, forcing my hands to come down on the wall of leg bones to catch myself.

They're a lot steadier than I expected. Where I had assumed it would feel like a fragile Jenga tower, wobbly and unstable, they're so tightly stacked that it doesn't even budge. When my knees are just above the wall, I bend them and press my kneecaps to the remains, being careful as I walk my hands out past the long, smoke-colored tibias and femurs and onto the pile beyond. I feel Dean let go of my ankles and look up. I'll only have to crawl out into the moat of skeletons just a little ways to reach one of the light fixtures.

Being as careful as I possibly can, I creep across the remains, trying not to think about the fact my hands are landing on human pelvises, feet, digits... Oh God, what is that? A vertebra? "Just keep moving," I whisper to myself, and a few more paces forward, I'm directly under the light. I stand up on my knees, walking my hands up the stone wall, and when I'm balanced, I reach for the clear cover across the light source. Whatever the material, and whatever they've used as the bulb, it's surprisingly cool. I was expecting it to be hot after being on for so many hours. I get my fingernails between the ceiling and the cover and pull. It pops off with ease.

I try not to look directly into the bright bulb, and reach in to figure out how to disconnect it. Feeling around, there's a small box between the bulb and the stone, so I grasp it and tug gently. The whole thing comes out in my hand, the only thing remaining a tiny black cord I now see strung between the lights around the perimeter of the chamber. It hadn't been visible from the ground.

I call down to Dean, "I've got it, but there's a little cord attached."

"Just pull it out. It's what connects all of them to the solar panel they're attached to outside," his voice echoes from below.

"It won't turn the light off?" I clarify.

"No. Once it's disconnected, we'll still have a good five hours of light out of it," he assures.

"And once I disconnect it, will it make all the other lights shut off?" I question nervously.

"No, love. They're all separate fixtures. You probably can't tell, but each one gets a cord of its own, they're just strung together so you don't see them from the ground," he promises.

In this moment, it dawns on me that I love how patient he is with me. He never rushes me, never brushes off my questions, never seems put out when I ask a million of them. And when he answers them, he's never condescending. There's so much I could learn from him, and he'd be such a wonderful teacher.

"You got it, Em?" he calls up to me.

I pull the cord out of the small box attached to the bulb, and all the lights, including the one in my hand, stay on, just as he promised. "Got it!"

"Awesome. Now, get back down here. I don't like not being able to see you." I barely make out that last part, as if he wasn't saying it to me, but more to himself, yet with the hollowness of the chamber, his words drift up to me, blanketing me and making me feel protected, cared for… loved.

It's a little harder to crawl across the bones on my knees and only one hand, but eventually I get to the edge and peek over the side, seeing him looking up while he waits for me. I smile down at him.

"Well, hey there, beautiful," he says softly, a gentle smile of his own playing on his lips.

"Hi," I reply dumbly. "Now how do I get down?"

"Hand me the light," he instructs, holding his hand up. I reach down and place it into his open palm, watching as he takes it to the open doorway and sets it on the ground, not taking the time to look inside before hurrying back over to me. That makes me pause again. He didn't sneak a look into an entrance that hasn't been open in over a hundred years. Instead, he rushes to stand below me and lifts his arms, saying, "Okay, now sit on the edge then jump down to me. I've got you, love."

I don't even hesitate. Like a reversed trust fall, I gingerly lower my butt to the leg bone outer wall and then launch myself off. Dean catches me with ease, and I wrap my legs around his waist, my arms around his neck, and then kiss the ever-loving hell out of him. I don't know what comes over me, but I take over his lips like a woman possessed, and I don't stop, even as I feel him move. The next thing I know, my back is against the stone wall as he grinds his hardness against my throbbing heat. He breaks our kiss to move his mouth to my neck, trailing upward to the sensitive place behind my ear.

"God, what are you doing to me, woman?" he growls low against my flesh, making me shiver.

"I'm… I'm sorry. I ju—"

"Fuck, don't apologize. I love it. Scares the shit out me, but I love it," he whispers, pressing his forehead to mine as he continues to thrust against my core, the seam of my jeans setting off fireworks behind my closed eyelids. "I want you so fucking bad. I want to lay you down and kiss you all over. I want to taste you again. God, once just wasn't enough. So perfect for me. Between the best sex of my life and our flawless connection, I would keep you forever."

I don't know how to respond. No one has ever spoken to me like this before. Anything I say won't do justice to what I'm actually feeling on the inside. Treasured, precious, wanted, beautiful, unselfconscious… almost powerful. His words strengthen me, and for once I don't care about looking awkward, or feeling silly or worry about if I'm doing something correctly. I just want to *feel*. Feel what he's doing to my body, and what he's repairing inside my very soul.

"As much as I want to fuck you right up against this wall," he breathes, "I don't know how much time we have left before they get us out of here. By now, they have to know I'm trapped. I don't want you to miss your opportunity to make your first of many great discoveries. And I have no doubt, love, as fucking brilliant as you are, there will be many, many more. I'm just happy I get to be with you for your first."

He kisses me one last time then sets me to my feet, taking my hand and leading me toward the door. I pick up the light and step inside the doorway, taking my first look around.

"A mausoleum," I exhale, taking in the three walls of floor-to-ceiling white marble, separated into row after row of tombs by vertical and horizontal lines of gold, each burial chamber marked with a golden plaque. Two walls, the one to the left of us and the one straight ahead, are separated into casket-sized tombs, and the one to our right is made into a grid of much smaller squares. I assume this wall is more a columbarium, a burial place for urns full of ashes belonging to people who chose to be cremated. In the center of the room is a stone set of table and benches, looking like it had never been used before.

I make my way to the left wall, holding the light up to read the names written on the plaques, feeling Dean close behind me. "This must be the exclusive part of the catacombs. The part only the most rich and infamous knew about and could buy a resting place," he mumbles. "Guess they're not in the second tunnel after all."

We walk along the perimeter, reading from top to bottom the names of people I haven't a clue who they were, the dates ranging from the early 1800s to the 1910s, when the catacombs were sealed and forgotten. "The dates aren't in order, so I guess they didn't bury them in the order they died," I observe aloud.

"No, mausoleums are just like graveyards. You pick your own plot," Dean explains, and I nod. It's not until we have almost reached the end of second wall that I recognize a name.

"No. Fucking. Way," I whisper, spinning to face Dean and hiding the plaque behind my ass, my eyes wild with astonishment and excitement.

"What?" He grins. "What did my beautiful little genius discover now?"

"Since I can remember, it's always been a rumor that the tomb in St. Louis Cemetery Number 1 wasn't actually her *real* burial place." I pause for dramatic effect, enjoying the mirth dancing in his eyes. "Behold, Mr. Savageman. I give you… the final resting place of Voodoo Queen Marie Laveau," I say, and slide aside, allowing him to read the gold sign with her name and *1794 - 1881* engraved in the center.

His mouth drops open, and I'm so thrilled at what I found I do a pirouette, the light in my hand spinning along with me. When I stop, the name the spotlight lands on catches my eye, and I nearly trip trying to run toward it. "Holy *shit!*"

"You're kidding me. Who is it this time?" Dean chuckles,

catching my arm to steady me.

"*We're devils and black sheep, we're really bad eggs. Drink up me 'earties, yo ho,*" I sing. "*Yo ho, yo ho, a pirate's life for me!*" I hand him the light, jump away, and start doing the running man dance, watching him shine along one of the rows of tombs until he lands on the name.

"Jean fucking Lafitte," he hisses, and he turns to face me, where I'm now doing a combo of the running man with the shopping cart. "But he was buried at sea in the Gulf of Honduras."

"Apparently not. New Orleans was his favorite city. It makes sense he would be buried here. Either that, or we just found his missing buried treasure. *Yaarg!*" I exclaim, and launch myself toward him, kissing him soundly on the lips before taking the light back out of his hand and making my way to the wall of smaller tombs.

Each one is about six-by-six inches, and as I count, up and then across, I see it is twenty-five chambers high and thirty across. So many tombs. It almost looks like a giant wall of mailboxes when you go to a post office. Abruptly, my enthusiasm plummets along with my stomach, and I feel my happy smile fall as well. "How in the hell are we going to find this damn ring?" I murmur, stepping back and taking in this side of the room as a whole.

Suddenly, I'm exhausted, and I plop onto my ass, right there on the ground instead of the stone bench a few feet away, and stare up at the white marble grid. Dean comes to sit beside me, wraps his arm around my shoulders, and pulls me in to his side. "Don't get discouraged now, love. We're right here. It has to be here, in this chamber. All the clues have led us to this exact spot," he reminds me, and I let out a sigh.

"I'm just so tired." I look at the watch on his wrist, seeing it's well past six in the morning. I've now been awake for twenty-four hours, running on pure adrenaline for the past six since I got trapped in the tunnels with Dean.

"I know. I'm right there with you. When we get out of here, I just want to take you back to my hotel, curl up with you in my king-sized, fluffy, Egyptian-cotton-covered bed, and sleep for a week. After we shower first, of course." He kisses the top of my head then rests his cheek there, and my heart flutters at the thought of us showering together, and then cuddling up... in a bed... outside the catacombs. It's both exciting and terrifying at the same time.

"Dean, I..." My words trail off. I don't really know what to say to that. He always says such sweet, overwhelming things to me, and then my brain can't form the words to respond. But I need to. I need to find the words, because our time together in the catacombs will soon be coming to an end. "Soon, we'll be out of here. We're going to have to go back to reality."

"Yes. And...?" he prompts.

I don't look at him. Speaking my mind about this subject is tough enough. There's no way I'd be able to do it while looking into those amazing eyes.

"When... when we get out, things will go back to normal. I-I mean, I know you'll be with me through everything when we get rescued. Through the news reporters, and then everything about our discovery—"

"*Your* discovery," he interrupts.

I push my hair behind my ear and look into my lap. "*My* discovery. But then, after that. After that, I'll just go back to being me. Holed up in my room, working on my blog. I might get lucky and be allowed into sites, now that I have this under my belt, so yay for that. But still." I clear my throat, trying to find more words for what's inside my head. "Out there, I'm not brave. Shit, this is the first time I've ever broken the law. I've never broken a single rule my entire life. Out there, it's scary. The *world* scares me. The only thing that doesn't scare me is these abandoned, sometimes spooky places that would normally scare everyone else. And now that I think about it, maybe that's why I like them. Because no one else wants them."

I take a deep breath and confess the rest of my fears running through my mind. "You'll go back to being you. The rock star of documentaries. Chased by women everywhere you go. Girls constantly offering themselves up to you, completely public on social media, right there for the world to see." I glance up at him, a sad smile on my face. "You know, that's another rule in our drinking game. 'Take a shot every time a chick asks you to marry her while you Live Tweet during a new episode.' We had to change the rule from 'every time a girl propositions you,' because that made us drink way too much."

I gaze back down at my lap, not able to hold his stare. "I'm not like them. I'm not a flirtatious kind of person. I'm not brazenly sexy. I'm an admittedly socially awkward nerd who had to be told that your boner was caused because you actually *wanted* me. I'm… I'll never be like them," I whisper, feeling tears fill my eyes and trying my best to blink them back before they have a chance to fall.

"You done?" Dean asks, and his sharp but somewhat amused tone makes my eyes snap back to his.

"I—"

"Yeah. You're done," he cuts me off. "That's the last I'm going to listen to you put yourself down." He wraps his arms around my hips, and then lifts and spins me, sitting me down on his lap, my legs straddling him. I bite my lip, unable to meet his eyes. I don't want him to see how emotional this has made me. "You think I want anyone else?"

A tear falls, and I sniffle, mortified I couldn't hold back the damn feelings roiling inside me. I feel his finger under my chin as he tries to lift my face, but I turn to the side instead.

"Look at me, my beautiful, brilliant girl. Don't shut me out now," he begs, and it's the sincerity in his tone that finally draws my eyes to his. "You think I'm this womanizing, philandering libertine, and maybe I was once. But I'm not that guy anymore. Haven't been for a long-ass time. There's nothing out there—or inside one of these sites—that scares me more than the thought of losing you. From the moment I kissed you that very first time, felt you in my arms, how perfectly you fit against me... I knew there was no version of my life without you in it."

I suck in a breath, my lip trembling as fast as my heart is pounding inside my chest. "You... you can't possibly know that, Dean. We haven't even known each other a whole day. Relationships formed during crazy circumstances don't last. You don't even know who I am outside these catacombs. It's not a promise you can make," I breathe, the tears falling freely now, because what he said makes me realize the thought of losing *him* is scarier than anything else I've ever experienced before.

He stares into my eyes, the look of love so blatantly clear inside his that it takes my breath away, as he cups my cheek and uses his thumb to brush away my tears. And with the sweetest smile lifting the corner of his lips, he whispers back, "I just did, love."

THIRTEEN

DEAN

I'VE NEVER MADE A PROMISE I didn't intend to keep. I've also never made a promise to a woman before. I've never told someone I was dating that I loved them, because I've felt like I knew what love is. I saw it growing up with Mr. Watson and Miss Potts, and I never felt for a woman what I saw in the eyes of those two when they looked at each other.

Until now.

When I was young and would stand between Mr. Watson and Miss Potts, there was a swirl of feelings in the air. An electrical crackle soothed by a feeling of comfort and calm. Almost like the sting of alcohol being poured on a scrape, and then the immediate feeling of relief when someone blows on it. Worth the pain to feel that overwhelming reprieve.

It's the same feeling I get when I'm with Emmy. Not having been around it in years, it was easy to recognize. Like a familiar scent. I can't smell blueberry muffins without thinking of my college roommate, Lee, because he lived on them when he was studying for a big test. He had so many containers of them that it permeated the air of our dorm room. So now, whenever I smell anything blueberry, it takes me back to cram sessions with Lee, staying up late, crushing Red Bulls and junk food, even this many years later. I haven't been around that feeling of all-consuming love since Miss Potts passed away, but as soon as I had Emmy in my arms, there it was. But instead of sensing it between two other people, it was me getting to experience it firsthand, and it's a full-body experience.

My head is filled only with thoughts of her. My hands itch to touch her, whether to bring her the most intense pleasure, or just to feel she's really right here, within my reach. My heart pounds inside my chest with excitement, every moment spent with her filled with anticipation of learning something new about her. My stomach is full of butterflies, and they set off in flight every time she looks up at me with those hypnotic green eyes, which right now are filled with tears. But hopefully I've turned those salty drops of fear into ones of happiness at my promise.

She doesn't say anything, but I've learned that when something I tell her really affects her, she can't respond. It's like I steal the words from her mouth; she doesn't know what to say. But I can see her taking it all in, internalizing it, and storing it to keep for a while. She's not ignoring me. She's not blowing off the things I'm saying. She lets them live inside her, almost like they break apart into little workers that find her scared and broken pieces and heal and glue them back together again. I'll take that over flowery words any day.

The panic that had been written all over her face slowly fades. The exhaustion weighing down her shoulders seems to lift, replaced with determination. The light that had dimmed inside my girl suddenly flips back on. It's remarkable to watch. I've never been so tuned in to another person in my life. She gives me a nod, leans down to kiss me swiftly before placing her hands on my shoulders to help steady her as she stands, and then faces the wall of miniature tombs.

I place my hands on the ground behind me and lean back, tilting my head to one side to watch her as she walks up to the wall. She paces back and forth along the full length of it, stopping every once in a while to read a nameplate, squatting down to look at one below eyelevel, standing on tiptoes to read one up high.

She takes a step back, using her finger to count up then across. She tilts her head back, and I hear her mumbling, but can't quite make out what she's saying.

"What is it, love?" I ask quietly, wanting her to know I'll help her with anything she needs, but not wanting to disturb her train of thought.

"Twenty-five up and thirty across. How many tombs is that?" she asks, still facing the wall.

"Ummm…" I close my eyes and do the math in my head. "Seven-fifty," I reply.

"That's what I thought. So why is the very last tomb marked 749?" she questions the room. My brow furrows, and she turns to look at me. "This wall, the tombs are marked by a number. Still not in order by date, but each mailbox, basically, is numbered."

"I guess so they could find a specific one more easily, since there are so many of them," I suggest.

"So if it's in order, with tomb number 1 at the bottom over here,"—she walks to the far left corner that butts up against the back wall of the mausoleum—"and the numbers proceed up, then back down the next column, then up again, like a zigzag," she hurries over to the opposite side and points to the very last square at the bottom, "then that tomb should be number 750. Not 749."

"So let's find the missing number," I tell her, getting to my feet.

We meet at tomb number 1, and together, we start counting upward.

"One… two… three…" we murmur in unison, slowly taking a step back and using the light to illuminate each one of the boxes as we make our way higher.

"Fourteen… fifteen… sixteen… eighteen…" Our heads jerk to face each other.

"It jumps from sixteen to eighteen. Sixteen to eighteen, Dean. Sixteen-eighteen," she whispers, her eyes filled with incredulity.

"1618, love. You did it again. You fucking figured it out," I say on an exhale, but before I can swoop her up in a celebratory embrace, she takes off past me. I watch as she reaches one of the stone benches in the center of the room, grasps one end of it, and starts to tug. It barely budges, so I hurry to help her.

We drag the bench across the floor to the spot directly underneath the missing box, and Emmy hops up on top of it. "Holy shit," she hisses, then looks down at me. "You have to see this."

Careful not to knock her off the bench, I step up and hang onto the wall to discover what's got her so excited. And then nearly fall off when I see it for myself. In the same gold separating all the tombs into a grid, the line separating the boxes marked 16 and 18 is actually a row of Atlantean rings, their triangles lined up point-to-point across the width of the column. Unless you were up here, looking at it straight on, you would never see it from the ground.

"How do we get it open, Dean?" she squeals, unable to contain her excitement, and I feed off it.

"We need something to fit in the cracks between the rows," I say, jumping down and looking around the chamber for a flat rock, or anything we could shimmy in.

"Dean, my purse. Grab my knife out of my purse," she tells

me, and I glance up at her with a surprised look. "What? I love my city, but some areas aren't the safest, especially at night, when people like to get wasted."

A feeling of pride that she has that protection with her mixes with a feeling of anger at the thought of her ever having to use it swirls inside me. But as she calls, "Dean!" it snaps me back into action, and I run to grab her bag, still out in the chamber of bones. When I return with it in hand, I hold it up to her, not wanting to scavenge through her things. Miss Potts taught us boys a long time ago to never go into a lady's purse.

She rifles through it, my anxiety growing with every second she takes to find the knife. "We're going to have to fix this," I growl.

She glances up from her giant red bag to meet my eyes for a moment before continuing her search. "Fix what?"

"What's the point of you carrying a knife for protection if you aren't able to get to it quickly when you need—"

"Got it!" she interrupts, paying me no mind as she takes hold of the strap of the purse and lowers it gently to the ground beside us, turning to face the tombs once again.

A conversation for another day, I suppose, but soon. I set aside my aggravation and hop back up on the bench with her, only for it to return tenfold as I watch her struggle to get the knife open. Jesus. If she were attacked and needed the damn thing, even if she found it in time, it'd be useless, since she can't even get the fucker open. I wrap my hand around her trembling ones as her own frustration starts to show.

"We'll be talking about this later, love," I warn her, my tone deep as I hand her back the open knife.

"I haven't had to use it since my dad brought it back as a souvenir from Egypt when I was seventeen. It's always in there as a just in case. Never had to open it before," she explains quietly, looking up at the tomb she's about to open. "I have a whole actual set of dig tools at my house. I wasn't expecting this adventure or I would have grabbed it on my way out the door."

At least I don't have to worry about her slicing her hand open. With her degrees and parentage, and how careful she was with all the clues and bones, she knows her way around an archaeological dig. I have no doubt she'll do her best not to damage the tomb nor herself.

I watch on with bated breath as she sticks the tip of the knife in the crack between the first and second column of marble cubbies. Placing her hand over the square of marble marked 18, she wiggles and leverages the knife, gently prying until the side finally pops up, and she catches the tile in her left hand before it even has a chance to move an inch. She turns just enough to place the square of marble and the knife into my hand before facing the mailbox-sized opening.

She lifts her hand to reach inside, but then stops herself. Glancing over her shoulder up into my eyes, she asks, "What if it's booby-trapped? Or cursed? What if—"

"Em, our tattoos, remember? You got this, love," I assure her, fully believing in the power of the symbol, and she nods. I step directly behind her on the bench, my feet planting on the outside of hers, and I reach my arms out to brace myself, a hand on each wall, forming a protective cocoon around her in case something scares her and she jumps back. Part of me, the alpha in me, wants to check and make sure nothing is in there to hurt her, yelling at me to lead the way to keep her safe. But this is her discovery. I don't want to take this experience away from her, so I grit my teeth and wait as she reaches her delicate hand inside the yawning space.

"It's open," she tells me excitedly. "There's no bottom in the eighteenth tomb. It combines with the sixteenth below it to make one big box." She leans up on her tiptoes to reach down inside the tomb, feeling around the bottom of the sixteenth. When she finally stops rifling, she lowers onto flat feet, slowly pulling out a box made of a cream-colored stone.

"Calcite," she breathes, as if reading my mind. "It's one of the same materials Egyptians used in making canopic jars. Where they stored the organs when mummifying the deceased."

I hop down, wrap my arm around her waist, and set her on her feet on the ground, then pull her to sit on my lap when I lower myself onto the stone bench. "You ready?" I prompt, as she holds the box in the palm of one hand and lifts the other to the lid.

She takes a deep breath, blows it out, and then nods. Fitting her fingernail in the tight crack, she pops it open and pulls off the white top, handing it to me. She tilts the box carefully toward us, and there, sitting in the bottom, just as all the clues had led us to believe, is the Ring of Atlantis.

"Do you see it too, Dean?" she whispers, as if the sound of her voice could make it disappear. "It's really in there, right?"

"Yeah, Em. It's really in there," I assure her quietly, letting her take it all in.

"I'm scared to touch it. I don't want it to fall apart," she confesses, her eyes locked on the small white ring made of sandstone, afraid to look away from it.

"You don't have to touch it, Em. It's your discovery. You found it," I tell her gently, and I feel her relax against me for a moment before she stands, taking the lid from my hand and carefully putting the box back together. She grabs the strap of her purse sitting on the ground next to the bench and carries it over to the stone table in the middle of the room, setting everything down so she can untie her jacket from her bag. She lays it out flat on the table, folds it in half, and then folds the sleeves over the body, making it into one long rectangle. Placing the white box at one end of the fabric, she starts to gently roll it until it's completely wrapped up inside, then takes it over to the sparkly backpack I'd set just inside the doorway when I'd gone to grab her purse for her. Securing the pull string and then the button, she places it back on the ground with great care before turning back to me.

And before I know what's happening, she's rushing toward me where I still sit on the bench, and then she's on my lap, straddling me, kissing me like she needs me to breathe. My arm comes around her hips and I yank her against me, her blistering heat coming to rest directly on top of my pulsing hard-on. I stand and she wraps her legs and arms around me as I walk up to the table. Grabbing her purse, I set it on the remaining bench, leaving the tabletop clear to first set her ass on the edge before lying her back. It's the perfect height to grind my rock-hard cock against the wetness I feel through her jeans as I reach between us to cup her, pulling a whimper from her as she shoots her hand behind my neck to pull my lips back to hers.

Gone is my timid, skittish kitten. In her place is a woman so engrossed in her passion for me that I let her do what she wants. I feel her other hand lift the edge of my shirt and then her not-so-gentle touch as she caresses my abs and chest, making my hips instinctively thrust against her. God, she's maddening. And then she's yanking at the fabric, desperate to pull it off me. I break our kiss and stand up to take off my shirt, watching as she sits up to do the same, and then to my proud astonishment, she bravely unbuttons her jeans and slides down the zipper.

"Help me, Dean. Get them off me. I need you," she whispers, lying back, lifting her hips, and shoving her jeans down. I step back, pull off her Converse, grab ahold of the snug fabric around her ankles, and yank, and the skintight denim comes off, along with her panties. "Now yours," she instructs, the urgency filling her voice and face causing me to jump into action. I swiftly shed the rest of my clothes, and I've barely stood to my full height when her legs wrap around my hips and one arm comes around my neck, hauling me down on top of her.

I've never felt more desperately needed in all my life as our lips connect once more and she reaches between our bodies to take my painfully hard erection in her hand and guides it toward her soaking wet entrance. And with her ankles locked around my ass, she fills herself with my cock, letting out a whimper before a sigh of relief. I feel my eyes cross behind my lids, her blazing heat feels so perfect.

With frenzied movements, our moans and breath echoing off the marble walls of the enclosed mausoleum, along with the smack of flesh against flesh and the sound of her wetness, I take her almost violently, her urging me on with digging nails and strong legs pulling me against her as she meets my every rough thrust. She's made me lose control, but as I watch her face, there is nothing but utter bliss written on her features.

"Oh, God," she breathes, and her brow furrows, her lips part, and her head turns to the side to press her face into my bicep as I rest my elbows on either side of her. I feel her hands slide up my sides and around my back to eventually hook onto my shoulders and she then lifts herself enough to bury her face in my neck. With my left elbow down to balance me, I slide my right hand down across her throat, feeling her clench around me. Something to explore later. It travels lower, squeezing her breast, before making its way down her side and finally beneath the small of her back so I can lift her enough to pound into her, making her scream out in ecstasy.

"I'm coming," she cries into my neck, and her grip on my shoulders tightens, her nails digging in as she explodes, causing my own orgasm to detonate. I groan loudly, shuddering against her, hearing her sexy moans as she continues to come around my cock.

I lay her back, kissing her gently, sweetly on the lips as she comes down from her high and her trembling legs begin to relax. And that's when we hear it.

It starts as a low rumble. And then the rumble gives way to loud, mechanical noises and the sound of rocks smashing into other rocks. I pull out of her gently, kissing her stomach as I bend down to pull up my underwear and pants wrapped around my ankles. She sits up quickly and then wobbles, putting her hand to her head, and I reach out to steady her. "Don't move so fast, love."

"What is that, Dean? Did we make more of the tunnel collapse? I... I couldn't be quiet. I'm sorry. I wasn't paying atten—"

"No, Em." I take her face in my palms and kiss her gently. "We're being rescued."

Emmy

WE COME OUT THE unmarked door on the front of the building disguising the catacombs' entrance to a sea of flashing lights, from both cameras and attached to police cars and fire trucks. Dean's arm is firmly around me, so I can't run.

"I've got you, love," he says against the side of my head, kissing me there. But it does nothing to soothe me. I'm about to go into full-on panic mode.

So many people. So many sirens. So many news vans with cameramen standing next to reporters with microphones and all dressed up in business suits or dresses.

Dean guides me up to where Mr. Hosea is giving an interview. I recognize his voice from when I hid behind the door. God, was that really just yesterday? It feels like months ago.

"—pretty easy, because only the entrance to Tunnel 3 was blocked. A little help from a jackhammer and a pulley system and we were able to move the boulders out of the way. Oh, here they are now! Found these two right as rain touring the tunnel, just waiting for us to discover they were stuck inside. Doesn't look like they had a rough night at all. And it turns out, the little lady found something pretty interesting…"

And as all eyes and cameras turn on me, the world goes black.

FOURTEEN

Emmy
Two months later

WHEN WE ARRIVE AT CHARLES de Gaulle International Airport in Paris, Erin and I are greeted at baggage claim by a handsome, muscular man in a nice gray suit and dark shades, holding a sign with my last name on it. He offers us paperwork showing he's with the Louvre security, so we know he's not some stranger there to kidnap us. He helps us with our luggage and escorts us out to a huge, black Mercedes SUV, lifting our bags into the back without breaking a sweat.

About forty-five minutes later, Erin and I both staring out our windows with our mouths hanging open at the breathtaking buildings and monuments we pass by, we pull up to a door situated in a large building with multiple storefronts. Looking at it from the outside, I would have never guessed it was a hotel. But sure enough, as the security guy tells us in his delightful French accent to go ahead to check in, when we walk in through the narrow doorway, it opens up into a small but super fancy hotel lobby. The reception desk is directly to our left, and straight ahead are small bistro tables and chairs, and a buffet to the area's right, where it looks like a continental breakfast is offered. It's empty now, seeing as it's nearly two in the afternoon.

The floor is made of white diamond-shaped marble tiles in sets of four, with a smaller black one in the center of them. There's a huge crystal chandelier in the center of the ceiling, and the reception desk is a luxurious dark-stained wood, with golden pens mounted every few feet for people to use to fill out their paperwork for their stay.

"*Bonjour, Mesdemoiselles,*" the pretty brunette behind the desk greets.

"*Bonjour,* ça *va?*" I reply, asking her how she's doing. My dad always told me the French aren't as rude as people make them out to be, as long as you show them you're at least trying to use their language.

"*Très bien, et vous?*" She tells me she's very good and asks the same.

"*Bien. Parlez-vous l'anglais?*" I answer that I'm good, and then ask if she speaks English.

"*Oui,* yes. How may I help you?"

"We have reservations for the next week. *Je m'appelle* Amelia Crain." There. I've used up all the high school French I can remember, telling her what my name is. Hopefully it's enough to keep the pleasant look on her face.

"Ah, *oui!* How exciting to have you, *Mademoiselle!* I just didn't expect you to be so, eh… eh…" She circles her hand in front of her, looking for a word to use. I have no idea what her line of thinking is that pertains to what she thought I'd be, but I'm relieved when she goes with, "… young. How wonderful for you to make such a tremendous discovery at such an early age."

I'm taken slightly aback by her knowledge of who I am, and she must see it on my face. "*Oui, Mme.* Crain, you are all over the news. Everyone is *très, très* excited to have a newly discovered artifact as an addition to the world-famous Egypt section of the Louvre. Not to mention one with such a fascinating history. The unveiling gala was sold out in less than twenty minutes, and tickets were well over five thousand euros! You'll be mingling with some of the wealthiest people in the world in a few nights."

This makes me a little nervous. I didn't think the gala was going to be that big of a deal. When my parents made their discovery in Egypt, they only had a small dinner thrown in their honor. Of course, their discovery wasn't an artifact that could be put on display in the most famous museum in the entire world. And the bit about mingling with the wealthiest people… Erin and I only brought little black cocktail dresses with us, and it sounds like the event is going to require much fancier attire than that. I guess it's a good thing we are in one of the fashion capitals of the world. Looks like we'll be making a shopping trip on the *Champs Elysées*.

"*Monsieur* Savageman checked in yesterday, but he is out at the moment," the receptionist says, snapping me out of my thoughts, and nervousness overwhelms me at the mention of Dean's name. God, I have no idea how I'm going to react when I actually see him in person again. It's been two months since we were rescued from the catacombs, two months since we'd made love… two months since I told him I couldn't be with him, since I saw the most heartbroken look I've ever seen on another human being's face, made worse by the fact I was the one who put it there.

And yet he hasn't relented. The flowers still come like clockwork. The gifts still show up on my doorstep. The calls still ring at all hours, even though I always ignore them, and similar voicemails are left every time. "*Amelia, please talk to me. I miss you.*"

And when he found out I was coming to Paris for the unveiling, the addition of, *"I can't wait to see you, love, whether you feel the same way or not."*

I feel a mix of both relief and disappointment that he's out right now. I'd fully expected him to be waiting for me, here in the lobby when I arrived. Thankfully, I'd been distracted by the beauty of the city, or I might've had a panic attack on the way here.

"If you can just sign this, and then here are your two keys. They reserved you one of our suites. *Monsieur* Savageman and then his producer are in the other two. We put you on the same hallway, as requested."

A little squeak makes its way out of my throat before I can stop it, and everything in me wants to tell her to move me to a different floor, but I don't want to bring unnecessary attention from her or my best friend standing right next to me. So, instead, I use one of the fancy gold pens attached to the desk to sign for the room, take the key cards from her, hand one to Erin, and place the other one in my hoodie's front pocket.

"*Monsieur* Doré, will you show these ladies to the lift and to their room, *s'il vous plaît?*" the receptionist asks our driver from the Louvre security, and then to me, she says, "He is here to escort you the entire length of your stay here in Paris, your own personal bodyguard. Anywhere you'd like to go, just ask."

I turn to him, and ask, "Doré? Doesn't that translate to Golden?"

He nods and gives me a slight smile, taking hold of the handles of our suitcases. Man of few words, but he definitely looks like he's fit for the job of bodyguard. I have the fleeting thought of what a coincidence it is to be assigned someone whose name means Golden, when I'm here to unveil the discovery of the lost Ring of Atlantis, a symbol shaped by The Golden Ratio, but I shake it off as Erin and I follow him to the tiny elevator past the bistro tables.

The elevator car barely fits the three of us with all four of our suitcases, but we manage to squeeze in awkwardly until it arrives at our destination on the seventh floor. We file out into the hallway, find which direction our room is according to the arrow on the wall in front of us, and head left. The hotel is much bigger on the inside than it seemed on the outside, so it surprises me how long we have to walk down the corridor to reach our room, 737. My mind briefly wonders which room Dean's is, but I don't let it linger.

I hold the key card up to the electronic panel above the knob, the light turns green, and Mr. Doré pushes the door open before grabbing the handle of two suitcases that have two more attached with clips to the front. He leads the way inside and gracefully manages the luggage over to the wardrobe in the back corner of the room.

"This is a suite?" Erin whispers next to me, and we both look around the small room, which is smaller than a normal room at a Holiday Inn. Even the accommodations in little bed-and-breakfasts around New Orleans aren't this tiny. Where Americans are used to two double-beds or one king-sized as options around the US, it looks like we get two beds that are not even as wide as what we call a twin. But the room itself is gorgeous. Everything is modern, decorated with stark-white bedding, silver fixtures, and sleek black wood—not at all what I was expecting from the antique look of the lobby, elevator, and hallway.

I move back to the door we passed on the way inside to take a peek into the bathroom. No tub, but it has a beautiful floor-to-ceiling glass-encased shower, and lighting over the vanity and sink that I'd kill to have in my bathroom at home.

All-in-all, it's much smaller than what we imagined, but I truly love it. It's cozy, and I know I'll be comfortable here to rest in between all the touring I plan on doing while we're in Paris.

"Thanks for all your help, Mr. Gold," Erin says, holding out some cash to the quiet man I now see is Asian, since he took off his sunglasses in the dimly lit room. She glances back at me and wiggles her eyebrows. I hold in my laugh at what she called him. My bestie is probably giddy as hell saying the name out loud to someone, since she's completely obsessed with the show *Once Upon a Time*. She sidles closer to him, and I pull my lips between my teeth to keep from giggling at her antics as she reaches out to feel his beefy bicep. "Oh, my goodness. So strong. You must have to work out for hours every day," she flirts.

His face remains stoic, but he lifts his hand to push the one offering the tip away, and his accented voice comes out deep when he tells her, "No gratuity necessary, *Mademoiselle*. Everything has already been taken care of."

She pockets the money and now wraps both her hands around his bicep, tossing her hair over her shoulder with a practiced swish of her head. "What gorgeous eyes you have. Where are you from?"

He gently and politely removes her hands from his arm, and replies, "The better to see my husband with, dearie. And my family is Korean, but we moved here when I was a baby."

I hide my laugh behind my hand and a cough, and watch Erin's face morph from flirtatious to pouty. Poor girl looks like he just peed in her Cheerios.

"Well, thank you, Mr. Doré. I think we'd like to shower and get the travel funk off, but if you could come get us in about an hour or so, we'd like to go shopping for something more suitable to wear for such a big event," I tell him, and he nods.

"You have four other guests arriving this afternoon. Tonight, there is a small dinner with all of you at the Louvre, and then the unveiling is tomorrow evening," he informs me.

"Four guests?" I question. "I know my parents are flying in, but who else is coming?"

"Oh, I'm sorry, maybe they are Mr. Savageman's guests," he replies, and my heart plummets to my stomach. Who could be coming for Dean? He never travels without his entourage, so they're most likely already here with him.

Is… Could one of them be another woman?

Mr. Doré clears his throat, interrupting my thoughts as the butterflies inside me turn frantic and start running into the sides of my stomach, making me queasy. "I will return for you in one hour. If you'd like, you can meet me out front. It will be the same SUV you arrived in."

"Thanks, Mr. Gold," Erin pipes up, and she plops onto one of the beds when he shows himself out. "You all right, Em?"

"Yeah, I-uh… I'm just worn out from the trip. I'll be fine once I shower," I lie, going over to one of my suitcases to get out my toiletry bag.

"Uh-huh," she mumbles. She curls up on her side and tucks herself around her pillow. "Wake me up when you're done with the shower."

"Will do," I tell her, and lock myself in the bathroom. Turning on the water, getting the temperature just right, I do what I've done for the last two months every time I'm alone and thinking of *him*.

I collapse under the hot spray, wrap my arms around my legs, and cry.

"Patrón, s'il vous plaît," I tell the waiter, as Erin and I sit alone at the table set up in the center of the Egyptian section of the Louvre.

"Er, we don't have that, *Mademoiselle*. We do not have the full bar set up yet, like we will have at the unveiling tomorrow. But we do have a selection of wine," he explains, his British accent lending some relief that I won't have to fight through a conversation. "And I can make sure your drink of choice will be here tomorrow evening."

"Thank you. I'll take a glass of whatever sweet white wine you have," I tell him, and Erin orders one too. "Just keep it coming too, if you will. It's going to be quite a night."

"Of course," he agrees with a smile, and then disappears out of view.

After shopping for four hours on the Champs, finding a dress for tonight, and then a gown for tomorrow, we didn't even have time to go back to the hotel to change again before dinner. We paid for our clothes then changed into them in the store's dressing room, our hair and makeup still looking fine since we'd fixed ourselves up before Mr. Doré picked us up.

When we arrived at the Louvre, he escorted us inside. It was actually quite creepy, since it was almost completely empty of people and most of the lights were either turned off or dimmed. He led us to the Egypt section, where a long table with twelve chairs was set up, a white tablecloth covering it, and tea lights down the center. Erin and I chose two seats next to each other and sat down, and now sit alone, waiting for everyone else to arrive. I am shaky and miserable. I'd had coffee but nothing to eat, because I had a nervous stomach, knowing I'd be seeing Dean, and there is no way to avoid it. And God only knows who his guests are. The thought makes me vomity.

"Baby girl!"

My head snaps up from where my eyes were staring into the tea light directly in front of me, and a small sense of relief washes away some of my jitters. "Daddy," I breathe, then "Mom!" when she walks in behind him. I stand up and rush into his arms, and Mom wraps her arms around us both.

"There's our girl," Mom says, her voice filled with love and pride. "Congratulations, sweetheart. We're so excited for you."

"Thanks, Mom," I tell her, my face heating at the attention.

"We're the first to get here?" Dad asks, looking over my head to see Erin waving from her seat at the table. "That never happens. We're usually late for everything."

"Yeah, we were a few minutes early since we came straight from shopping. We would've been late otherwise. Nobody else has arrived yet," I say, but then in walks Mr. Hosea, Nox, and a man I don't recognize.

"Emmy, m'doll. Nice to see you again, dear." Mr. Hosea holds his hand out to my dad. "Chase Hosea."

"Ah, nice to finally meet you. I just have to say, sir, you are a good man for what you've done for my daughter. It takes a great person to allow all this to happen, under the circumstances," Mom says, and he turns to shake her hand as well.

"Hey, I give credit where it's due. That ring and all of those tombs would have never been found had she not been down there. The entrance to Tunnel 3 in the catacombs has already been repaired and everything is as it should be. Emmy deserves her time in the spotlight, whether she wants it or not," he chuckles, referring to how I fainted when Dean and I were first rescued. "We're not going to have a repeat of that, now are we?" he asks, looking at me.

"I hope not, sir," I mumble, and turn to smile up at Nox. "Hey, big guy." I walk up to him and give him a hug. We'd become pretty good friends over the last couple months. He brought me my camera—which was full of all sorts of pictures of everything going on inside the catacombs—when I stayed the night in the hospital the day after my big adventure. They wanted to keep me for observation, even though Dean had apparently caught me before I hit the ground. They gave me fluids through an IV, ran lots of blood tests, and a full check up to make sure we hadn't breathed anything terrible in when the tunnel entrance collapsed. Turns out, I hadn't destroyed the entire main chamber like I thought I had. If Dean had run to take cover in either one of the other two tunnels, or up the stairs, when he picked me up, we could've walked right out of there, no problem. But then, none of this would've ever happened. It all still feels like fate.

"Hey, little bit." Nox crushes me to him then sets me back on my feet, and I turn toward the man I haven't met yet, holding out my hand.

"Hi there, I'm Emmy," I introduce myself, feeling pretty proud. I've been practicing for the last month and a half, when I realized that living so close to the catacombs after the news of what happened broke and what I'd found meant I would be recognized constantly. I hid in my room for a couple weeks, but then Erin dragged me out. She pointed out I wouldn't be able to hide forever, and started preparing me for the big reveal here in Paris after Mr. Hosea contacted me, letting me know all the details of what would be happening to the Atlantean Ring. She's learned all sorts of techniques in her psychology classes to help people with anxiety, and I could feel them actually working.

"My boy wasn't lying. You are quite beautiful, Amelia. My name is Watson," the older gentleman says, taking my hand in his, flipping it over, and placing a quick kiss to my knuckles before engulfing it with his other hand.

I gasp. "Mr. Watson?" My heart races, and my knees almost buckle. "I-I... it's so good to meet you. Dean told me so much about you when we got... um, when I made the... well. You know."

He chuckles. "Yes, I know what you mean. And he's told me all about you as well." He leans down so only I can hear, still holding my hand in his. "He's been a wreck without you, dear. Like you've stolen part of his soul." He stands back up and gives me a sad smile before turning to introduce himself to my parents.

I make my way back over to the table, feeling like a zombie, plopping down next to Erin, and absently taking note when Nox sits down on the other side of me. I don't know what to think about what Mr. Watson just told me.

"Right here for you, little bit. You need me to run defense, I got your back," Nox grumbles low.

"Thanks, big guy," I whisper.

Mom and Dad take seats at the end of the table, Mr. Watson sitting to the left of them, and I assume Dean will want to sit next to Mr. Watson, since I'm blocked in on both sides, which will put him directly across the table from me.

Fuck. There will be no hiding from him.

Mr. Hosea chooses a seat on the opposite end, leaving room for five more people, Dean included.

Suddenly, the sound of footsteps echoes off the quiet museum's walls, and my stomach plummets. Heels. It's clearly the sound of a woman's high heels clicking rapidly through the entrance, and I cannot bear to see who Dean has brought with him. I have no right to be jealous. He's made countless efforts to see me, to get me to accept him. But I just couldn't. The day we left the hospital, we were met outside the doors by hoards and hoards of women vying for his attention. Begging for his autograph and to take pictures with him. And when someone's disgusting panties flew past my face, I was done. I knew I couldn't handle Dean's fame, so I ran. I jumped in a cab and made it to my house, locking the door behind me.

He'd camped out in front of my house for days, but being a good best friend, Erin hadn't let him in, even though she scolded me tirelessly for turning him away, especially when I wouldn't tell her what happened between us. Eventually, he had to move on to his next location, seeing how the production on the catacombs episode would have to be put on hold until the tunnel was repaired. But then the flowers and gifts had started showing up. Every. Single. Day. And still, I refused him.

I hold my breath, clenching my nails into my palms, fighting the urge to run right out the door without ever looking at who Dean has brought. And right as the lights start appearing before my eyes from lack of oxygen, that's when I hear the guest's voice.

"Hey, girl, heeeeeeeey!"

I jerk in my seat, my brow furrowing, and my head snaps to the room's entrance. And there, next to the most handsome man my eyes have ever laid eyes on, the one who made my body and soul come to life… stand Ricky and Calvin.

I stand so abruptly my chair falls over, and the loud crash reverberates throughout the room. But I don't have time to feel embarrassed, because my feet are moving, and before I realize I've even stood up, I squeal and launch myself at my two best friends I've never gotten to meet in person before this moment. The guys sandwich me between them, and the three of us jump up and down like a bunch of teenage girls, yelling, "Ohmygodohmygodohmygooooooooooood!"

When we finally pull back, tears are running down all our smiling faces. "What are you guys doing here?" I exclaim, holding my side that aches from all the exertion.

"Your hunky pursuer teamed up with your girl-bestie, and we flew in to surprise you for your big day! An all-expense paid vacay to Paris? Yaaaassss!"

I hear Erin's heels clicking as she comes up behind me, and I spin toward her, giving her a quick hug before turning to Dean. I force myself to meet his eyes, and immediately feel an electric current zap through my every vein.

"Thank you, Dean." My voice comes out in a croak, so I clear my throat. "Thank you." This time, it comes out quiet but clear, and his face softens.

"You're welcome, love," he replies, his voice deep and gentle, blanketing me, wrapping me up in warmth and comfort. We stare into each other's eyes for a long moment, no one and nothing in the entire universe existing except for the man in front of me, the one my soul is crying out for as it reaches for its other half.

"Giiiiiiirl, I bet Beyoncé doesn't get the Louvre all to herself! Hashtag-take-that-Kim-K!" Ricky exclaims, breaking the trance Dean put on me with those multi-colored eyes and that perfect, gentle smile he seemed to reserve just for me, not the show-stopping grin he gives everyone else.

I smile up at Ricky, and then remember, "But I thought I heard high heels coming into the room." I look around the three tall men, but no one is with them.

"*Psh*, biotch, please. You heard my bling-for-days cowboy boots, baby," he singsongs, and strikes a pose to show off his rhinestone-encrusted teal boots, the heel at least three inches thick. "I've been saving these puppies for a spesh occasion, and I read in an article on Facebook that people in Europe think everyone in America is from Texas and dress like cowboys. So I thought I'd be patriotic."

"I tried to tell him that not everything he reads on Facebook is true, but you know how he is," Calvin grumbles, but his eyes are full of mirth and love for his husband.

Sigh, hashtag-relationship-goals, I think, and then realize they're looking at each other the way Dean, the man I fell for in the catacombs, looks at me. I could have that. I know I could. But I know myself, and I know I couldn't handle the constant attention surrounding Dean Savageman, the celebrity.

"Shall we?" Dean holds one hand out toward the table, and wraps his arm around me to place his other at the small of my back, sending a shockwave up my spine and down to the tips of my burgundy toenails.

I manage to stay on my feet, even though I wobble on my strappy heels, as I loop my arm through Erin's and we get back to our seats. As expected, Dean sits next to Mr. Watson, right across from me, and Ricky and Calvin on his other side.

Finally, Mr. Doré enters the room, followed by a man I haven't met. But by his expensive suit and air of intelligence, I assume this is probably someone very important.

"*Bonsoir*. My name is Jean-Luc Lenoir, Chief of Louvre. Thank you for coming to my little museum for dinner tonight," he welcomes us with a grin, and we all chuckle.

"He speaks English so well," Ricky points out to Calvin, but a little too loudly, and we laugh as we all hear Calvin kick him under the table. "Sorry, guys. My ears popped on the airplane, so if I start yelling at you, I promise I'm not mad."

Mr. Lenoir laughs lightly, and explains, "I'm fluent in English, Spanish, and Greek, and I can hold my own in Italian if they don't speak too quickly. But thank you. You're too kind."

They fill the remaining two seats at the table, and as if they'd been waiting in the shadows for their cue, four waiters appear, the original one setting glasses of wine in front of Erin and me.

The night is passed with amazing French food, lots of laughter, stolen glances across the table—quickly darted away every time I saw Dean was staring at me, except the one time I caught him giving Nox a death glare when I laughed at something he said—and just a constant outpouring of congratulations and pride. I'd never felt more accomplished in my life. All the hard work I'd put into school, all those times I was shut down and turned away at different sites, all that disappointment… it was all worth it. I was surrounded by every friend I have in the whole world and my loving parents, having dinner with the head of the most famous museum on Earth, and it was all happening because I'd found and put together the clues to make such an amazing discovery. And what made it even better was to be sharing this night with Dean. Even if I was terrified of his lifestyle and couldn't actually *be* with him, I was so happy he was here.

When conversation died down, bellies full of French onion soup, beef burgundy, and chocolate mousse for dessert… and lots and lots of wine… Ricky and Calvin were the first to slide back from the table.

"Best night ever, honey. But we are beat after that flight. We will see you tomorrow," Calvin tells me, and I stand and meet him at the end of the long table to give him and Ricky hugs goodnight.

"Where are y'all staying? Do you need a ride?" I ask, about to offer to let them ride with Erin and me in Mr. Doré's SUV.

"We're staying at the same hotel as you, but we've got our own yummy chauffeur," Ricky says, gesturing to the door, where a handsome bearded man wearing a black suit stands. "Apparently, it's part of Mr. Doré's interview process to hire only the hottest of security guys."

Mr. Doré clears his throat and stands, turning with a smirk. "That's actually my husband, and yes, that was one of the stipulations on the application."

We all laugh, glancing to where the other Mr. Doré is now shaking his head, face blushing, with an embarrassed smile lifting the corners of his lips.

My parents are the next to rise from the table, and then Nox and Mr. Hosea. And seeing I'm not sitting back down, Dean nudges Mr. Watson, tosses his napkin onto the table, and scoots his chair back. After hugs and kisses from my mom and dad, who exit with their own chauffeur, the rest of our group makes our way out the front door of the giant glass pyramid.

"Shotgun!" Erin yells, skipping to the front passenger door of Mr. Doré #1's SUV.

"Why w—" I start to ask why she wouldn't be sitting with me

in the back, like we had been the entire time since we'd arrived in Paris, but cut myself off when I realize Mr. Watson and Dean are still with us.

The head of security unlocks the vehicle with a remote, and without waiting, Erin opens the door and hops in, shutting it behind her, and gives me a wicked grin through the glass. I stare daggers at her and scratch the side of my nose with my middle finger.

Mr. Doré opens the back door and gestures inside. When I just stare at him awkwardly, then glance between Mr. Watson and Dean, he explains, "Being head of security, I am assigned the guests of honor. Mademoiselle?" He gestures inside again, and I finally force my feet to move. I step up inside and move to the very back, to the third-row bench seat, sliding all the way to the driver side. And just like I figured he would, Dean joins me in the back, Mr. Watson choosing to sit in the middle row, in the passenger side captain's chair.

My heart begins to pound at Dean's closeness. As we start our way to the hotel, it feels like someone sucked all the air out of the SUV, and I'm left taking short, quick breaths, trying desperately to get enough oxygen into my lungs. The walls of the vehicle begin closing in on me, and I feel my knees and hands start to tremble. *Nonononono, not again...* I can't tell if my whimpered chant is inside my head or out loud, but just as I'm starting to get tunnel vision, everything going black around the edges, I feel an arm wrap around me like a lifeline, and Dean's familiar scent fills my lungs, making it possible for me to finally take a breath. My body naturally melts against him, and as my vision clears and my shaking eases off, I feel tears prickle the backs of my eyes. I want to blame my weepiness on the several glasses of wine I had with dinner, but I know that's a lie.

God, to be in his arms again. I can feel this is where I'm meant to be. A sense of completeness washes over me, and my head lays on his shoulder of its own accord. "I'm here, love," Dean whispers, bending his face near mine, the scruff on his chin lightly brushing my cheek.

No one else in the car even notices anything was amiss. The three of them are having a conversation about… I don't even know what. I can't make myself care enough to put forth the effort to pay attention to their words. Dean doesn't try anything else, just holds me for the rest of the car ride, and for that twenty minutes, I push out everything telling me I can't handle being with him, and just let his presence soothe my soul. For the first time in two months, I feel like I'm home. And I know that's weird, since I've been right there, hiding in my room as often as Erin would allow, but here, in Dean's comforting embrace, my body pressed snuggly into his side, this… this is where I feel the most at home.

I want to cry when the SUV finally comes to a stop in front of our hotel's entrance. I'd give anything for Mr. Doré to just keep driving… drive until we run out of gas, and then fill us up and keep on going. Instead, he opens the two passenger side doors, and everyone lumbers out, Dean stopping to turn and hold out his hand to help me down. As my fingers slide against his palm, I never want to let go.

But when I stand to my full height as I step out on the sidewalk, Erin loops her arm through mine, barely gives me time to say goodnight to the three men, and hauls me toward the elevator. "I have to pee so bad everything looks yellow," she declares, dancing in place as the door slides open and she hustles us inside.

I'm in a daze. All I want to do is run back into Dean's arms and tell him I'll be with him. But that stupid niggling voice that taunts me, reminding me of those swarming people outside the hospital doors, the pictures of him with his fans tagged on Facebook and Twitter, everything that pulls up on every social media outlet when I search #DeanSavageman, all the lewd and dirty comments people leave under his pictures… I just… I just can't.

The door of the elevator opens, and we step out onto our floor. Erin reaches out to press her hand against the wall, using her other one to slide off her stilettos, and lets out a relieved groan. I follow suit, my ankles practically sighing.

"This, Em, just so you know, is better than sex," she states, wiggling her blue-painted toes a moment before we continue down the hallway to our room.

I snort. "Hardly." As soon as the word is out of my mouth, my eyes go wide and I slap my hand over my mouth, risking a peek over at my best friend, who looks taken aback.

"Excuse me?" she gasps. "What aren't you telling me, *bestie?*" She almost looks hurt. "Please tell me how pulling those godforsaken four-inch torture devices off your feet isn't better than your one and only horrifying sexual encounter." Her arms cross over her ample chest, and she juts out a hip and starts tapping one bare foot as her heels dangle from one hand.

Damn you, wine! Me and my big mouth. There's no avoiding telling her everything now.

I throw my head back and groan, looking up at the fancy light fixture attached to the ceiling. "Fine. Shit. Let's get back to the room and I'll confess all," I whine.

"You're damn right you're confessing all. I knew something went on in those catacombs you weren't divulging," she rambles, as we walk the rest of the way down the hall to our suite. I pull the key card out of my clutch and wave it in front of the electronic lock, and when the light turns green, I push down the handle and lean my weight against the door, dragging my feet, not wanting to have this conversation.

We both toss our heels onto the floor and start stripping, ready to get out of these uncomfortable dresses and confining undergarments. When we've peeled off the Spanx and traded our strapless bras for comfy pajamas—mine being a mid-thigh-length tee with gauze-wrapped mummy hands covering my boobs that my mom sent me from Egypt—and Erin finally pees, we each sit on the edge of our beds, facing each other, sitting Indian-style.

"Shoot," Erin demands, and I take a deep breath.

"Where do I even begin?" I grumble.

"How about starting at the part when we went to bed that night, and I woke up to the news station reporting that your arch nemesis was trapped in the catacombs, and you were nowhere to be found in our house," she gripes.

So I do just that, telling her everything, in detail, from my Snapchat conversation with Ricky and Calvin, to my sneaking down into the tunnels, to yelling at Dean and making the entrance collapse, all the way up until the point where we found the clues leading us to believe the Atlantean Ring was buried in there with us.

"And… well… somewhere along the way, I didn't hate him anymore, and I realized he was actually this really amazing man, one who hadn't deserved all my wrath." I feel the corners of my lips tilting upward thinking about him. I stare out the window at our awesome view of the Eiffel Tower, but I see right through it, my mind's eye focusing on nothing but Dean's beautiful eyes, and that sexy smile that melts me now, rather than making me want to do him physical harm. God, how I've missed him.

"Earth to Emmy! And then what happened?" Erin prompts, and my eyes meet hers and immediately tear up. I watch through my swimming vision as her face transforms from huffy to confused to understanding, as if the proverbial light bulb turned on in her pretty head. "Oh, my God, Em—"

"Yes." I nod frantically, and she launches herself from her bed to mine and wraps her arms around me. "It was… God, it was amazing, wonderful… like the man himself. I fell for him down there. We made love, like, literally. We created *love* in those catacombs. It was as if we were made for each other, and everything had led us to that exact spot at that exact time, and we were trapped down there until we figured it out. But…." My words trail off and I shake my head.

"But what? Why are you just now telling me this? If you feel this way, why aren't you *with* him right now? It's been nearly two months, and you haven't said a word about the man. That's how I knew *something* was up. In the last two years, there has never been a single day where you didn't make at least one snide comment about Dean Savageman, and then you guys got rescued out of there, and *bam!* Not a word. If you're in love with him, why the hell have you been avoiding him?" she questions.

"Because, Rin! You *know* who he is. *Everyone* knows who he is. He can't walk ten feet without someone asking for an autograph and a selfie with him. You saw me on the news. Just two minutes in front of all those cameras, and I fainted, right there for the world to see. I'm way too much of an introvert for all that attention. It would never *work*," I sob the last word, wishing I wasn't so much of a loner freak so I could be with the man my heart aches for.

Suddenly, Erin stiffens and gasps. "You asshole!" I turn my tear-streaked face up to look at her with confusion. "All those flowers, gifts… all the ignored phone calls. Those were from Dean! They weren't from the museum like you said, were they?"

I sniffle. "A couple of the phone calls were from the museum, and one from Dean's producer, but yeah… the rest were f-from D-Dean," I stutter through sobs, remembering all the wonderful, thoughtful things he sent me that I forced myself to ignore.

"Bitch-move, bro," Erin tells me, disregarding my crying. "Right now, I'm going to let you off from telling me all the good, juicy details of catacomb nookie. We'll save that for later. Instead, it's time we have a little talk, and if it comes to it, I'm physically going to knock some sense into you."

My brow furrows, nervous of what she's about to tell me.

"Since we were little, you've always hidden yourself away. You've been so focused on your schooling, your blog, your career, that you've literally had four friends your entire life, and two didn't even really count until now, because you'd never even met them in person. I've been your hetero life partner since we were kids. And although I've loved every single second of that title, woman, we're twenty-four. I mean, we aren't freaking spinsters or anything, but if you've found this man... one you're obviously completely head-over-heels for, then you shouldn't let him get away just because you're afraid of his celebrity status." She shakes her head, letting that sink in a moment.

I don't know why, but something urges me to feed into her speech, giving her even more ammo. "We have matching tattoos." I look up at her again and see her eyebrow arch. "I never knew he had it, because he always wears long sleeves on the show, but he has my exact tattoo on his forearm." My French manicure-tipped finger traces along my own skin, where his ink was wrapped around his ripped arm, remembering how I had traced it after we made love.

"So you're telling me that out of the infinite number of symbols, sayings, pictures, or whatever, in the entire universe, the man you got trapped down in the catacombs with, in which y'all made this great, huge discovery, just so happens to have your exact same tattoo, which you grew up with all over your house?" Her jaw drops as I nod and bite my lip to keep from letting any more tears out.

Her sudden and swift swat upside my head nearly makes me fall forward off the edge of the bed, from the surprise of it, rather than the actual force, although it didn't feel very good nonetheless.

"What the hell, Rin?" I whine, rubbing my head and straightening back into my Indian-style position.

"Yeah, exactly, Em! What the ever-loving hell is wrong with you?" she screeches. "Can't you see it's fate? Y'all are clearly meant for each other. Nothing else explains it. The woman who wants nothing more than to be an archaeologist for locations here in the US, but who has a vast amount of knowledge of all things Egypt because she's the daughter of famous Egyptologists, gets trapped down in the New Orleans Catacombs with the rock star of American history documentaries. And when their nerdy powers combined, they were able to make one of the greatest discoveries in the history of ever?" Her voice is excited as she flails her arms about.

"Well… I don't know about the history of *ev*—"

"The fucking history of ever, Em!" she cuts me off. "People have been looking for that ring for over a century! And *you* found it, woman. *You.* Your first time finally making it into one of these goddamn locations after two years of begging, pleading, and flashing your tits—"

"It was one time!" I interject, but she ignores me.

"—and you use tiny, impossible little clues to figure out that the Ring of Atlantis, the very symbol you both freaking have permanently tattooed on your bodies…" She hops up onto the bed, jumping on the mattress and making me bounce to my feet between the beds. I can't help but smile up at her antics. "…is down there with you, basically screaming, 'Please! Find me, bitch! Get me out of here!'"

She leans down and grabs both my hands, hauling me up onto the bed with her, forcing me to jump along with her. God only knows what the people below us are hearing. And then something hits me, and I stop bouncing abruptly, the look of shock on my face surprising Erin into halting too, as she asks, "What? What is it?"

"One of the properties of the symbols, Rin. Intuition, the most mysterious of the three. The other two being protection and healing. The ones who wear the symbol become sensitive to certain communications they wouldn't have otherwise been aware of. It increases your intuition and ability to connect with higher levels of consciousness, and what some people believe are Spirit guides." When she gives me a confused look, not quite picking up what I'm throwing down, I make it clearer. "When have you ever known me to throw caution to the wind, and be like, 'Yo, I'm going to break into this secret location, since I got told no once again'? Never. That's when. But something possessed me that night. I didn't even give myself a chance to think. I was in the bathtub, for God's sake. And my happy ass got out, got dressed, and hauled ass to those catacombs like a woman on a mission."

An all-white grin spreads across my best friend's beautiful face as she realizes I'm trying to tell her that I'm starting to believe her fate theory, only it's backed up by my belief in the Atlantean Ring's power. "You've got to go to him, Em. You've got to get over this fear of the limelight and go get your guy. He's meant to be yours," she conveys, squeezing my hands between us.

I hop off the bed, looking around the furniture for where I unconsciously set down my hotel key card, but stop as Erin clears her throat. I glance up at her with a questioning look.

"Um, Em, you gonna wear that?" she asks, her eyes staring at my chest.

I look down, seeing my breasts being fondled by mummy hands, and jump, forgetting I had changed into pajamas. "Shit!" I squeak, and run over to my open suitcase, rummaging through before slipping on a pair of houndstooth-print leggings and a super soft, long-length black tee. I find my black flip-flops in the zipper pocket and slide them on my feet, then turn and grab the key card off the desk before hustling toward the door, stopping as my hand touches the handle.

I spin to look at Erin, disappointment suddenly coming over my face, until she says, "738, babe. He's right across the hall."

"How did y—"

"I asked Mr. Gold." She smirks and flips her hair over her shoulder.

I run and jump up on the bed, smack my lips against her cheek with a loud kiss, and then hurry back to the door and open it. "I love you, my hetero life partner," I call, hearing her laugh as it closes behind me.

I pause for a moment, leaning back against the door to my room, and stare at the one directly across the hall. My heart pounds in my chest, as if it's trying to break free and run away.

But everything Erin and I just talked about fills me with bravery, enough to keep all the doubt at bay, and I take the two steps forward to knock on his door.

FIFTEEN

DEAN

I STEP OUT OF THE SHOWER, wrapping one of the towels around my waist then using another to swipe over my hair a few times, running my fingers through it to guide it back into place. I toss the extra one over the shower door then turn out the light to the bathroom. Just as I'm about to step into the bedroom itself, there's a light knock on the door.

I grasp, turn, and pull the handle, fully expecting it to be Watson, who has a tendency to come chat before he goes to bed, but standing there, framed in the doorway, her hand still up in the air from where she was knocking, is my beautiful Emmy.

Her eyes go wide and her cheeks flush as her gaze falls to my bare chest, then lower, where my towel wraps low on my hips. I feel my dick jump at her attention, and her brows lift before her eyes snap back to mine.

"I uh…" She doesn't say anything else, just continues to stand there, hand still raised, and it's not until I see her fist start to tremble that I move.

I open the door wide, wrap my arm around the small of her back, and haul her against me, lifting her so I can step back inside to close the door then press her to it. Her shaking stops and I feel her relax, her small body growing soft as it molds against my front. Her reaction surprises me, as it did on the way back from dinner. As much as she's ignored and avoided me, it's not the response I expected from her.

I cage her in with my arms and press my forehead to hers. "What are you doing here, love?" I breathe, trying to keep the emotions out of my voice. I've tried to stay strong since the moment I saw her at the Louvre. I've done my best not to show her the mess of a man I've become over the last two months without her.

How much she had upturned everything in my life. Two episodes have been filmed since I last laid eyes on the love of my life. Production was slower than it had ever been. Countless takes having to be made, because my mind would suddenly go blank on what I was supposed to be talking about, and then all that would fill the empty space was our time down in the catacombs. I had never heard the word "Cut!" so many times on a single location, and it was all because I couldn't concentrate on anything but the sheer terror that filled my girl's face when all those people and cameras turned toward her after we were rescued. Or the look of—what was that? Hurt? Jealousy? Anxiety?—something, that came over her perfect features when we were met by a crowd of my fans outside the hospital. I didn't know, and it was one of the things that spent time circling inside my brain over and over and over again. Along with the vision of her fleeing as I gave in and signed autographs for a couple kids there with their mom. By the time I realized she left my side, all I saw was her dark hair disappearing into a cab at the taxi stand before she was ripped away from me.

If it weren't for Mr. Watson, God knows what I'd look like right now. He forced me to eat and work out with him every day, keeping to my usual routine. On days I didn't want to do anything but sleep the time away, he dragged me out of bed.

I'm whipped. I know it, but I don't care in the slightest. After finding her, I don't give a shit about much else. All I want in the world is to be with her. Part of me wanted to be mad at her. And an evil voice in my head wanted to make her into a bad guy. *She left you, just like your mom did.* But I couldn't. She warned me. She told me her fears right there in that hidden mausoleum. She'd confessed everything that scared her about being together outside the catacombs. So I couldn't hold any sort of grudge.

Finally, she speaks, and it's the sweetest sound I've ever heard. "I'm sorry, De—"

My lips crash down on hers, both my hands coming up to hold her neck and jaw as my tongue slides between her lips, hearing and feeling her sigh. All the emotions I've felt over the past months without her come pouring out of me in that kiss. I show her, rather than tell her, how much I've missed her, how much I want her, how much I *need* her. And as she reaches up to wrap her arms around my neck, what little control I have over the feelings rushing inside me snaps.

I lift her, her legs instinctively wrapping around my hips, and my hand moves to cushion the back of her head right as I slam her back against the door. It's like I can't get close enough to her. I grind against her, my towel coming loose and falling at my feet, and I can feel her heat so close, her soft, thin pants doing nothing to hide the fact she is wet for me.

She whimpers, and I pull back to let her catch her breath. Her eyes meet mine, the look of desperate passion in their depths matching what I feel on the inside.

"I have to tell you something," she whispers, and I shake my head. I don't want to hear her words. I'm too scared she'll tell me to stop, that she'll tell me she can't be with me and just wanted closure or some bullshit. No, I don't want to let her speak, so I lean in to kiss her again. But she turns her face away, squeezing her arms more tightly around my neck. "Dean, please. Let me tell you before I lose my nerve," she begs, and I close my eyes and nod, holding my breath and tensing to take the blow. "I love you."

My brow furrows and my eyes slowly open to meet her gaze. Unshed tears glisten there, but her face is full of tenderness. "What?" I need to hear it again, to make sure I hadn't just heard what I wanted to.

She blinks her watery eyes, and I watch her focus move from mine, to my lips, then back up again, a smile tugging up one corner of her full lips. "I love you, Dean," she says quietly but clearly. "I don't know how I'm going to deal with all the attention, all the crowds of fans always surrounding you... but I'll figure out a way. I can't... I can't keep crying myself to sleep every night. I can't keep seeing your face everywhere, knowing that you want me, and me be the only reason we aren't together. Do you..." She glances at my chest, hiding her face as her hair comes down like a curtain. "Do you still feel the same way you did in the mausoleum? Do you still want to be with me?"

I lift her chin to meet my eyes then move her hair out of her face, tracing her lower lip with my thumb. "I never make a promise I don't intend to keep, love," I tell her, and press a tender kiss to her lips. "I love you too, Emmy. I've never told anyone that before, and I mean it to the depths of my soul. I've loved you since the very second I held you in my arms that very first time in the catacombs. Maybe even before then, when I walked in on you dancing around the chamber. I love you, Em," I repeat, and she lets out a sound that's half-sob, half-laugh, but her face shows nothing but relief and happiness.

"Now that that's all clear," I lean forward and whisper against her ear, knowing she loves to feel my breath there, "I'm finally going to make love to you…" I pull back to grin at her, watching her smile spread, as I add, "In a bed."

EPILOGUE

Emmy
Two years later

Surrounded by Dean, my parents, Erin, Nox, Ricky, and Calvin, with the added bonus of my new friends Mr. Watson and Mr. Hosea, I managed to make it through the unveiling gala without a hitch. There were a few times I started to feel overwhelmed by all the attention, but Dean seemed to sense it before I even realized it was creeping up on me, and held me close until the feeling passed. He likes to say he's so in tune with me because of our Atlantean Rings, but I have a feeling there's a little more to it than that. I believe in soul mates, and on top of that, I know with everything in me that Dean is mine.

At the end of that gala, Dean's producer pulled us aside. He had an offer for me I never saw coming, and with our relationship being so new, I knew for a fact he didn't propose the job just because Dean and I were together.

"*Action!*" the director calls from across the cave, snapping me back to the here and now.

"I'm Dean Savageman," my love says, hanging from his harness above my head, smiling down at me.

"And I'm Emmy Savageman. And this is…" I turn toward the camera to speak my line.

And in unison, we say, "No Trespassing."

THE END

NOTE FROM THE AUTHOR

For the past year, Jason, my husband, has had to live four hours away for work, only getting to come home to his family on the weekends. I've had lots of nights alone to fill, and most of it has been with work-it just so happens I have my dream job, editing romance novels. But on those rare nights, when I finished my work early, I would scroll and scroll through Netflix, trying to find something to binge-watch. One night, something caught my eye I had never seen before. Mysteries at the Museum? Rarely having time for TV, I don't bother with cable, so I had never watched this Travel Channel show before. But hey, I freaking love museums, so I gave it a shot. I'd just watch one episode to see if I liked it. Next thing I knew, I was on episode 8. I had stayed up until 3 in the morning hanging onto every word out of the handsome and intelligent host's mouth. Yes, not only did I have a newfound love of history, but I also had a new crush: Don Wildman. Come to find out, he was the host of quite a few Travel Channel shows, so when I finished devouring every episode of Mysteries at the Museum, I started on Off Limits. And that's when inspiration struck: The cocky, sinfully sexy TV host. The beautiful, sweet, and smart introvert with big dreams, who hates his guts. Something happens. They're trapped together. Somewhere underground, maybe? They have to work together, and end up making a huge discovery. And somewhere along the way, the enemies fall in love. I still had to write Wish Come True, book 3 in my Blogger Diaries Trilogy, but it was such a relief when nearly the entire plotline of No Trespassing hit me. After writing my real-life romance, I was scared I wouldn't be able to come up with a whole make-believe story. With my trilogy, I knew every character's quirks, every minute detail of the plot, every twist and turn… because it all actually happened! Would I really be able to turn around then and use my imagination to create a love story worth reading? In my heart, I believe I have. This time, I wanted to write what I personally like to read: Instalove. The alpha male and the quirky girl who needs a little bit of saving. A hero with a heart of gold, even though he may not show it on the outside, and the heroine who is actually worth a lot more than she realizes. Adventure. Soul mates finding each other. True love's first kiss. And even a little bit of magic.

Dean and Emmy have filled me with so much joy, laughter, and heart-warming moments over the past few months, and I hope you enjoyed reading their love story as much as I loved telling it.

ACKNOWLEDGEMENTS

First and foremost, thank you to my hubby and girls for letting me hunker down in my cave and do what I love. Even though I'm not one of those Pinterest queen, Stepford wife kinda moms, y'all still love me, encourage me, and are proud of me just the same. It fills me with so much joy when my girls tell anyone we meet, "My mommy is an author," with a look of wonderment on their beautiful little faces, like I'm some kind of superhero.

Don Wildman, this book was dedicated to you, but I also have to say thank you. When I messaged you on Facebook to tell you about my story, I never in a million years thought you'd actually reply! But then you also generously offered any help I might need when it came to behind the scenes of TV production, and even sent this little fangirl an autographed picture. Thank you so much for that brilliant brain of yours. You inspired one hell of a hero.

Laura Crain, my reader/fangirl turned one of my best friends on the planet. Emmy is 90% you, my love. Smart and gorgeous with quirks you can't help but to love. My birthday weekend you came to spend with me inspired so much of my story. Not only Emmy's personality, but also the part I was missing from the plot. What the hell were they going to discover down there? I had no idea. But then you randomly showed me one of the bracelets you were wearing while we were strolling through the mall, telling me a little story about this dude who discovered King Tut's tomb, and how everyone with him had died crazy, mysterious deaths, but he was the only one wearing this symbol, this "Atlantean Ring", and lived to old age. And there it was. The final piece of the puzzle that was No Trespassing locking into place. Thank you for being you, because I wouldn't want you any other way.

Barbara Hoover, Rebecca Allman, and Mandy Pederick, my editing partners in crime, you girls are invaluable. Thank you for all of your hard work making sure NT is as perfect as it can be. Your daily encouragement, along with my PA Extraordinaire, Franci, was the boost of confidence I needed to get this done. Hot Tree Editing is my dream team, and the greatest group of women I have the fortune of calling my tribe.

Aurora Rose Reynolds, my Crystal-boo, what would I have done without you? I struggled so badly with my blurb, and you dropped everything you were doing to help me with it. And to impress the master of Instalove with my story, hearing you didn't want it to end… you have no idea how encouraging that is. Every day, I reminded myself of the advice you gave me so long ago-just get down your words, every single day. Even if it's just a couple hundred, get words on paper. We are an unbreakable team. Love you!

Marcia, I couldn't have written this without your amazing and intriguing website, www.atlantisring.net. You made me believe in the magic and power of the Atlantean Ring. Thank you for my gorgeous ring. I've worn it every day since you sent it to me, and I have no doubt it's because of it I was able to write this book in 19 total writing days. My words came so clearly, so thank you for blessing it for me! I hope my readers are inspired enough to come to you to get their own!

Ricky and Calvin McWells, y'all make the perfect besties for Emmy. I fell in love with Ricky the first time I ever watched his Snapchat story about his husband making him mow the lawn. So hilarious, so real, and he just downright made me laugh my ass off. And then he started doing stories about the love of his life, Calvin, and their furbabies, and I ended up falling in love with them as well. You guys have no idea how much positivity and happiness you brought into my life just by opening up and letting us followers into yours. With so much negativity in the world, your sweet, funny, and loving personalities are a light in the darkness, and it's exactly what introverted Emmy needed. It was just an added bonus that much later, after I'd already written these handsome fellas in my book, when I discovered Calvin has an armful of Egyptian tattoos! Seemed very much like fate was working her magic. So to the McWells guys, thank you so much for letting me include you in my novel.

Matthew Hosea, my Turd. You inspired so much of Dean's personality. Thank you for always taking time to answer my questions, when I'd come to you asking how a guy would react. You made me laugh so much, but then also blew me away with the care and charisma that came so naturally in your answers. (When I sent him Emmy's virginity horror story, Dean's answer was Matthew's verbatim: "What a fucking pussy." LOL) Your replies were surprising, and I was able to twist that shock into a new aspect of Dean's point of view, making him a unique character I couldn't have come up with on my own. It makes me look even more forward to the book we're writing together! #nerdandturd

And finally, thank you Sierra and Vaida. Y'all can't even begin to understand how much your messages meant to me. Would anyone want to read a romance with such a nerdy theme? But thank goodness you girls let me know there are a lot of people out there like me who love a good adventure along with their love story! And Stacia, as always, the best beta girl around. You will always have a place on my team. I'm sorry for making you throw your Kindle… again.

Made in the USA
Las Vegas, NV
01 July 2021